A WORLDLY TALE
TOLD OF
MOTHY CHAMBERS

by Kate Barnwell

Kate Barnwell

G
Grosvenor Artist Management

Other works by Kate Barnwell

Novella

'The Case of Aleister Stratton' by K.G.V. Barnwell

Poetry

A Collection of Poems & Lyrics
Ever Truly Yours - Reflections on Love

www.katebarnwell.com

A Worldly Tale Told of Mothy Chambers

First published in 2018 by

Grosvenor Artist Management
32/32 Grosvenor Street
Mayfair
London
W1K 4QS
www.grosvenorartistmanagement.com

ISBN 978-0-9935817-5-5

The night has a thousand eyes,
And the day but one;
Yet the light of the bright world dies
With the dying sun

The mind has a thousand eyes,
And the heart but one;
Yet the light of the whole world dies
When love is done.

Frances William Bourdillon (1852-1921)

Science Book
T. Chambers Class V.B

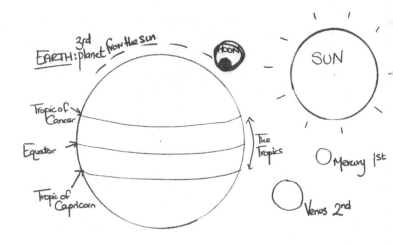

EARTH: 3rd planet from the sun

Tropic of Cancer

Equator

Tropic of Capricorn

The Tropics

MOON

SUN

Mercury 1st

Venus 2nd

MOON phases

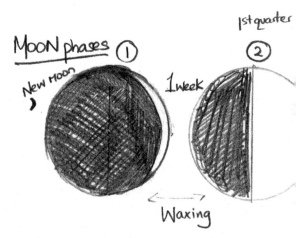

New moon ①

1 week

1st quarter ②

Waxing

Waxing: area of moon visible from Earth — increasing

As the Moon orbits Earth
the half of the Moon facing the Sun is lit.

The different shape of the lit portion
that can be seen from Earth
are the phases of the Moon.

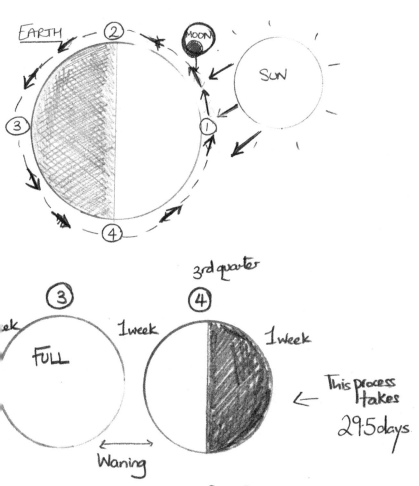

EARTH

② MOON SUN

③ ①

④

3rd quarter

③ ④

ek 1 week 1 week

FULL This process takes 29.5 days

Waning

aning: area of moon visible from Earth – decreasing.

Collioure, Languedoc Roussillon

April 2016

My dear Mothy

It's been a while since I wrote to you, I don't deny it. I'm sorry to have kept you in the dark.

You always assured me my letters would be forwarded to you wherever you moved. I cannot accuse you of being unsettled when I consider my own origins, although I see from the last postage mark, and on previous indications, you are now in a permanent residence.

This letter will be my hardest and my last. My hand is not as steady as it was but my mind is as sharp as flint. In these final months I have the most to express - a stretching of thoughts, a coming together of ideas, a transferral of truth. Why I find the more to say as I retire than I did with all the time given is, perhaps, one of the symptoms of society humanity has given me.

Philly passed away in January, an attack of bronchitis.
His lungs were weary. Christmas struck a bitter blow to his
chest and he conceded a gentlemanly defeat. Philly always
spoke frankly, often accused of being too candid with the
French and untypically English. His eager bright eyes and
busy thoughts suited the town he adopted - a city life would
have dulled such attractions and subdued that personality
which grew with each new meeting. I'll miss the honest
man I met those years ago. Still, it puzzles me how he never
guessed. The rumours of other worldly beings teased his
brain as did the wild possibility of life originating outside
the limits of Earth. With talk of spacecraft travel and the
Space Race competition between the Soviets and the United
States, he was like a child with a picture book. Not even on
his death bed did he confess an inkling of suspicion. Why
might I expect him to suspect something unusual of me
when I made no clear sign or habit of being so? The local
paper reports, even in a small Catalan town, were now
more questioning, inquisitive and philosophical over the
complexities of Space, the Sun and the Moon and the Earth.
There was new intelligence and new interest and focus in
the growing community circle which the landing of 21st June
1948 would not have received.

Often Philly shifted his attitudes and opinions – he was
wavering and indecisive on subjects, reading old books
and querying updated theories. He was once described,

unflatteringly as 'a waffler'. I think Madame Simkins would have loved playing with the French idiom, 'allonger la sauce' (to lengthen the sauce), speaking but saying nothing - but it's just not true, Philly had plenty to say and share. He believed in something beyond Earth, that's why we found each other. He had a passion and idea about Space that defied most people. He fostered in others a curiosity and imagination but failed to see what he trusted was right under his nose: me! I defended his integrity but kept the truth of my heritage and my arrival concealed, something I felt compelled to do. Maybe I closed the door on the customs of my origin, so eager was I to belong and participate in a new and peaceful province on Earth.

My ancestry, my parenthood, my extraction – they were hidden behind elements of truth and sincerity. Much of the relationship we quickly built together formed part of a social history on which we would focus our energies.

We didn't quite make our 50th wedding anniversary. You know it falls this September for it was the following month, the day I remember vividly, you dropped your little self onto our doorstep. How keenly you settled into our seemingly simple home. It was only 3 months; we each made our impression.

I have decided to return when the pod comes on the full

*moon of the Summer Solstice; the date is set for 20th June
2016. There is a space for me, there always is for a widow
and the rarity of its arrival and departure is an opportunity
I cannot forgo. Perhaps, quite practically, I need to explain
and convey the actuality of the circumstances from which
I came, something I should have done long ago. Does it
not resemble the sorting of attic boxes? Left alone to slowly
ferment until we find the safe and appropriate time, or
the moment of genuine courage, to face the long-postponed
decisions that must be made when we investigate the
contents. There is little point in resistance. Slowly, through
the years, more life and time is added to them and then a
lifetime of years have accumulated and we feel compelled to
finally take on what we had been hiding away to deal with
later. Well now is that 'later'. When a death claims the
heart, there is loss and sadness, then anger and loneliness
follow. I feel the emotions intensify. My pen is as keen as
my thoughts to channel the storm whirling inside my soul.
I must release the story of my provenance. I can only blame
myself for having repressed the truth.*

*The date of my arrival in Collioure is as clear today as the
first sea-shined pebble of the Mediterranean I saw that year.
It was the 22ⁿᵈ June 1967. I was 30. At last it was my
opportunity to land in the Northern Hemisphere of Earth,
our pod landing only occurs when a full moon falls on the
Summer Solstice. It is important you bear this in mind. The*

4

dates of such an appearance are so infrequent and I speak in terms of centuries. The Summer Solstice is the longest day of the year with over 17 hours of sunlight, but the rarity and exactitude of the two-combined make it an incredibly special event and a global phenomenon. The purpose of science is to develop systematic knowledge of the world through observation and experimentation. It strives to make sense of the universe and define it thus 'as a harmonious, orderly system.' The evidence produced in studies is intangible, we cannot touch it; we understand the cosmos in terms of theories and diagrams. It is not as confusing as it may appear, because we cannot grasp and see these complicated, vast areas of matter, relying completely on investigations, study and technology, it does not mean an awareness and knowledge of the galaxy is beyond our understanding. What the dispassionate scientist fails to see and remains oblivious to, is how a life elsewhere can harness certain extraordinary events in the Earth's cycle, taking the opportunity, they present, to enter Earth. I am sharing material with you now that many will never accept or believe: the ideology of extra-terrestrial life.

The Summer Solstice occurs when the tilt of the Earth's semi-axis is most inclined to the sun. The sun sits directly over the Tropic of Cancer, at the northern most point also known as the zenith, the highest point on the celestial sphere and the furthest point from gravitational force and

*the Equator. This explains the Summer Solstice of the
Northern Hemisphere: it simplifies the concept of its annual
occurrence. These are the reliable facts of science. Now let's
consider the habitudes of the moon, always an exception, a
curiosity: the gem of the skies whose path and performance is
an ever-changing peculiarity. It is the full moon, the perfectly
rounded mother-of-pearl balloon, falling on the Summer
Solstice, that is of specific importance to my landing. A full
moon occurs when the sun and moon are on opposite sides
of the Earth; the moon is in opposition to the sun. The full
moon rises as the sun sets. The sun is super high in the sky,
making the moon super low. Moonlight is forced through
thicker, more humid air and a glow of warm amber settles
on its surface. The two accomplish a remarkable scene:
a conception of beauty, power and influence. This honeyed moon, sitting ripe and sweet and heavy in the sky is a
paradisiacal sight: a moment, they say, only one life can give
you. It is at this juncture, when the sun stands still and the
moon is in its entirety, the pod of planet Ather enters Earth's
realm as fleeting as a shooting star. Such an episode as this
only accentuates the acute awareness of the brevity of time.*

*Philly wrote in his diary the night I arrived in this little
French town, 22ⁿᵈ June:*

*'The evening was hot, with a warm southerly wind, carrying
sands from the Sahara. The large, rose-tinted moon shyly rolled*

forward from behind the hillside, visible in the fullness of its glory yet lying low, sitting heavy in a pool of blue, there was a whisper in the air; a moment of change and new beginning. There is a promise and a hope I failed to see come with the New Year but appear to have gained from witnessing this singular event.'

He later said the effort to rise, as portrayed by the moon, had reminded him of himself: tired of the tedious, drudgery of the life he had left years earlier in the dreary, sprawling suburbs of London.

My dear Mothy, I always admired your steadfast loyalty and attachment to us. Your young innocence, so recently sprung from the world aged sixteen. Why you were almost half my age! You were more than a pen-pal and visitor, you were my continuing correspondent and, after Philly, your constancy in my life, though distant, remained an enduring comfort.

Tell your tale as you lived it Mothy. People will speculate, they may believe or disbelieve, that is the freedom of the mind. In whatever country or on whatever planet people dwell, if democratic, they have the advantage of freedom and speech. If life is corrupted or minds indoctrinated, a tale can be told and it can reach them but their suppressed unspoken thoughts belong to them, which without sharing, no man will know. This is not religion. I do not try to convince, only to share a tale, to make others see the world

7

around them is made of many men and women. Their eyes do the seeing, their mind the interpretation, if you alter or switch the angle then perchance a new vision is formed. All people exceed science; they are beyond its body of knowledge and discipline. We just work round it and make it work for us.

I give you this small jewel from 'Ather.' It sat on the mantelpiece from the day I married Philly. Please remember my life, my heart and my earth were always here.

Fondest love mon cheri

Philly's Belle and your **Bette** *x*

Part I

Let me begin with a simple introduction. Before you turn the pages of this book, you must meet and know something of the narrator; the handshake and chit-chat pleasantries of the printed word.

My name is Mothy Chambers, and my age and the date of our meeting today is not yet important. Read at your will and live as you do. In due course, I will frame the necessary years around my stories, for now our encounter begins unadulterated by times; we must not let numbers distance our friendship. You may feel inclined to ignore my tale if we do not partake in parallel lives or similar habits. Let its structure enlighten and entice you. As my steady voice is read through your mind and you follow the story as you would a rhythm, you'll begin to weave the threads of my personality into shape and assemble a character and his occurrence.

I'm an ordinary man with a few, faraway friends. You may find we have met before; they say a spirit has more than one life. However, it must be said I have passed enough years now to know cigarettes and fine wines are expensive essentials and how in the modern world I clearly suffer far too many vices for my doctor's approval. Her fresh-face and youthful mind seem to zap me of the energy I spend all night trying to restore. No-one makes green vegetables and hikes in the hills sound less appealing than a doctor chained to a desk with a port-hole of daylight. She woefully detests my dedication and susceptibility to the enjoyment of two daily diversions: tobacco leaves and the fermented grape. I tell her someone has to uphold the over-researched fashions of a past now heavily condemned. Full of the current framed medical facts and restorative thinking, she has not the originality to see how lives can be led by tastes and desires. Why it was decided that intoxicating sensual delectations should be our shortcomings and weaknesses baffles one so stimulated by them. My age pleasantly wraps me in the luxury of indifference like a youth's view of longevity. Should I live my life all over again I would do it the same way – I don't tell her this.

I was christened Timothy.

When my brother arrived and first coughed letters into decipherable words, he was unable to pronounce my already holy-confirmed name. He spluttered *'Mothy'* enthusiastically out of the crib, onto the table and into my lap; it stuck, and so remained, with friends and family alike, for the total of my 65 years.

Mothy Chambers became the name I lived my life by, with the exception of the time I travelled to France as a young language student.

From the age of seven I was a boarder at an old country boy's school: Battle-Gate, known by students as *'Rattlesnakes.'* The showers were fearfully cold and the rugby fields riddled with frozen solid stumps of mud.

The uneven desks with inkwells and squeaky school

chairs of unyielding Scottish oak bore the painful imprint of many beaten bottoms. School dinners were tepid and bland, made of only three colours, brown, white and sluggish green. These were the surroundings and formative feeding blocks of maturing young British men of the1960s. The decade of rock and roll and pop music never knowingly blasted onto the school grounds or exploded the walls or twisted and shook our souls. In secret we were caged canaries, uniformed and obliging, learning Bach and Beethoven until it was time to be safely released into a vintage social order. We were a generation type without the slightest knowledge or ability of how to live the life rapidly pestering the fringe of our parents' hierarchy.

By secondary level I was known as *'Toffee'* (it rhymed with Mothy) and formed friendships with my peers, particularly Lyme Matthews (we called him *Lymy*), Jeffrey Barker (we called him *Woof*) and Mole Feilding (we called him *Olly*). In class, few boys landed their true, motherly blessed names. They were given acceptable, sometimes challenging identities depending on their status among the ranks of the school fellowship, overseen by esoteric pupils. By and by, I mildly pity Richard Ogden-Cox, an ancestor of the apple family. He was faced with the tortuous nickname of odd Dick Cox with emphasis on the Cox. He blushed as red as a Royal gala every time it was sung in front of him.

My brother Nico joined me scholastically 5 years later; remarkably he remained Nico all through his school life. To this day I'm uncertain as to how he managed it.

When we came home during the long holidays my

father was consigned to his basement office. We used to watch him from the ground floor window moving a piece of paper from one side of his desk to the other, occasionally pausing, scribbling and then reflecting. Each year he seemed to lose more hair, until his receding forehead became a shiny bald pate. He worried about finances and stocks and shares. Mother not once lost her smile or her rag and since our schooling and home-life didn't change she jollied all his woes with copious amounts of homemade coffee cake and cheese scones and Sunday roasts, because food filled the gap where intimate conversation could not be conceived.

Moving swiftly along, I took a strong interest in the preservation of historic houses, estates and castles across the British Isles and was rewarded with a good income and comfortable housing: a keeper's cottage or a lodge with quaint rooms on site. This career, aligned with boarding school from a young age, completed my personal sense of self-sufficiency.

Our Trust consulted skilled artists, employing many craftsmen, often the last artists and restorers of century old traditions, zealously rescuing and preserving, from certain destruction, the beauty and style of an era damaged by age and regret and tax. They were known collectively as The Morris Branch in honour of William Morris, the inventive and socialist campaigner and pre-eminent member of The Pre-Raphaelite Brotherhood. In 1870, he had founded the *Society for the Protection of Ancient Buildings*. Morris seemed to embody the traits and characteristics of our talented group: a passion for design and craftsmanship, fiery tempers, an indifference to dress and disregard for social graces. At some point, we were all fervent believers in the romantic ideals of a utopian society. Essentially it was always considered an impractical and unrealistic scheme of perfection: an insurmountable task, especially after two World Wars.

The collection of socially and historically important structures slowly grew.

Olly had returned to his father's roots of iron mongering and welding; he was an invaluable contributor to our work. Lymy was called out many times to study the display of 17th century portraits hanging in the long galleries of over 20 estates. Woof joined the Royal Air Force but at the age of only 28 lost his life flying reportedly routine manoeuvres over the English Channel. A devastating and mysterious end neatly covered up. It was a loss that his superiors insisted brooked no further investigation.

I was told the school flag hung at half-mast for a fortnight. He was the only boy in the school's history to captain both the cricket team and the rugby team and win all home and away matches in single seasons. The prize for such glowing signs of leadership was to have his name inscribed on a silver trophy for *'Outstanding Contribution to Sport'*. He took much jovial stick for this achievement but bore it with the supreme good humour of the dignified sportsman he was. His loss reduced me to tears for the first time in my adult life.

I have lingered and deviated too long. We must rewind and return to 1967, I have reached the age of 16, when the world lay undiscovered. Suitcases were expectant and atlases were coloured patchworks: smoking with the air of the cities; sweet with the gardens of Eden; monstrous, salty seas; peppery, explosive mountains; unadulterated desert dunes and skies laden with mystery: black tingling with silver, blue dashed with white, and gold, striped with pinks and scented with orange.

Perpignan had been advertised as an excellent destination for young students to learn French; the exchange of money for the exchange of a bewildered English boy.

The journey began back in London; a sharp, cold, black morning. I was packed into a disordered coach with a school satchel and a small, brown leather suitcase. The early ride saw the night-parties still revelling in clubs and bars and the early-birds just beginning with newspaper under arm; each making use of the hour upon them. Then followed a rocky ferry ride across the English Channel. I shut tight my eyes, gripped my bags firmly, believing them to be both an extension of myself and a guard against my vulnerabilities. From Calais I was bundled into another dusty, swerving bus, smelling of French tobacco, with a small red-white-blue flag on the dashboard and a placard reading *'Paris.'* I took a long, jolting sleep until finally awoken with a smoky cry of, *'Paris!'* Subsequently, and giving great trust, I was briskly marched to another faded location by an old man with the gait and demeanour of one raged by his city's history. My chaperon, Jean, was paid for the ignominious job of gathering up and escorting across a crowded rush-hour city to *la Gare de Lyon*, one tired and overwhelmed English schoolboy.

The hotel, I guessed at, was titled '*Le Pension du Gare de Lyon.*" The '*Gare*' was missing a '*G*' and '*Lyon*' a '*y*' and very soon 'sion' would be invisible from '*Pension.*' The paintwork was peeling and revealed coatings of soot-stained grey, a black and a red. The sparse carpet was damp and smelt musty. The owner was Monsieur Alain. He smiled, exposing his three yellow dentures, I automatically and discreetly licked my upper layer of teeth, a reaction to spotting his gaps, while he stroked his greased back hair, gave me a key to room 5 and pointed a hairy arm upwards, '*en haut... la salle de bain est au premier etage.*' With a desultory shrug and a mumbled '*au-revoir,*' Jean thrust an envelope into my hands and shuffled out onto the street to continue his deeper resentments. The details for the following day were confirmed: I was to take the Perpignan train, ticket enclosed, due to depart at 7am, 500 yards from the front door.

I made the steps up to floor two. There were traces of other guests: a discarded toothbrush, a day-old newspaper, used tissues, a full ashtray, crumpled scraps of paper, a pressed shirt hanging on the banisters with an industrial smell of steam. The collection of dispossessed items, affiliated with no-one in particular but the generalness of the general public. They were pieces you might see on stage at the theatre for actors to act around. I skirted them. Room 5 overlooked a drab and ashen urban block. I drew the thin curtain, sat on the slatted single bed, put the pillow to my chest and then behind my back, cushioning me against the wall, and pulled out a packed meal from home. My last moments of bravery fell away, I sobbed quietly, briefly drying the hot tears on a white handkerchief, the one I had used to wave farewell. Once the emotion was spent I realised how empty I felt and how the cold was starting to embrace me. In defence, I munched on a slice of cold ham, a chunk of cheese and a sausage roll, the familiar foods of home. There were muffled shouts and heavy feet on the stairs. This was an overnight stay and temporary solution for the one night. I locked my door. Pigeons cooed outside the lunette and stirred in my dreams, for tomorrow *I* would be a bird flying south.

La Gare du Lyon station, the south-bound line, retained the dirt and sweat of travellers of decades. The air was miasmal. The sky was dense and saturated, punishing us all below with a thunderous downpour of filthy rain. At the start of the train journey, the weather washed over the windows, drowning my vision. I felt hesitant and befuddled by the less than eloquent confusion of trepidation and expectation.

The freshly-turned, bloody-brown soils of a bleak and rain sodden northern France came swiftly and poignantly into view. Only 22 years since the world ended its second fall into the misery of war. The hours turned, towns and hamlets came and went. Sleep consumed me, passengers arrived and left, one supplanted by another; they had no name to me, their faces bore no recognition, they were participants and wayfarers.

I felt the afternoon sun penetrate my eyelids as the train slipped rhythmically from a grey northern coolness to the welcome of the warm southern sun. The famed contrast Vincent van Gogh had discovered, producing his best and most famous art in the sun-drenched south. At some point, there is a divide and the country swops the heavy coat, labour intensive agriculture and the dejected spirit of the North for the light chemise, the hand-picked soft fruits and the vibrant, vivid days that symbolise the essence of southern climes.

The unconventional painter Salvador Dali, declared Perpignan station as the *'centre du monde'* (*'centre of the world'*). In the typical controversial fashion for which the unruly artist was both revered and scrutinised, he felt alerted to the station's aura by a bright shining light. He encountered *'a vision'* and *'a revelation'* and consequently he painted the surrealist work *'La Gare de Perpignan,'* in 1965, two years before my arrival. On his journey to Paris from his nearby native Spain he felt overpowered to stop at Perpignan station and send his luggage ahead by train.

On reflection of Bette's letter and those younger years abroad, many of these facts become increasingly fascinating, so much so I have purposely made some quick enquiries into Dali's way of thinking. Dali had a belief in the philosophy of cosmogony* (*a theory or story of the origin and development of the universe, the solar system or the earth-moon system). He believed in the strong presence of energy in this area. An unmistakeable gentle force seems to prevail upon your senses; your own persona seems capable of being different, of shifting slightly. When your body is situated on a new axis of Earth it has a new centre point, thereby switching your perceptions and the aura in which you operate (with insight, this makes a natural conclusion).

The city of Perpignan sits silently on the edge of the Mediterranean, in the bottom corner of the Languedoc-Roussillon region of south west France, claiming the tongue of the *Oc* or *Occidental;* the language of the west. It is the final major destination of France before entering the border of Franco's fascist Spain (1939-1975).

It is early October. Inappropriately I am dressed in long trousers, thick socks and a knitted jumper, my wool jacket has our school coat of arms emblazoned on the left breast pocket. I am a stranger to myself. The station platform at Perpignan was uncoloured and grim and for a long 5 minutes I looked to my left and right, searching beyond the rail lines into a distance from which I longed to be rescued. I've been deposited by train, whose wheels have sped the track of a 9-hour course. I felt disowned. The womb-like comfort and security wrapped around the train traveller is tangible, now abandoned on the platform I felt the lease of light slowly dimming and my eyes weakening. The warmth from my body had seeped into the carriage seat; in dull phases, it gave back patches of the recycled heat. Sleep, solitude and books had covered the majority of my rail journey until the landscape became that of the Cathars, of castles and *etangs:* captured inlets of saltwater. Vast fields pocketed with woodlands were interrupted by hilltop towns and their centrepiece cathedrals; a precipitous, abandoned castle seated on a jagged rock-face; the masterful rivers, and their minors, the waterways of trickling streams, rushed to the sea, all fed by melting mountain snows. This was my ever-changing vista. The knowledge I later gained I shall mix with the curiosity I first experienced, for knowledge and curiosity are not necessarily combined at the start of any new adventure. Please excuse the tendency to mix tenses. Sometimes I am right back where I started as a boy, other times I am the wiser writer, observing my younger self.

At 16 I knew I was not yet formed into a true mature self. I had not yet seen enough, or any of the world, to have answers, to ask questions or to find the questions to even ask. I had been secluded, organised and lectured from rooms to playing fields and now this healthy excursion would mark the beginning of my transformation into a world worthy gentleman and I looked to this world for healthy attributes and associations. I entered into its diversity ready to apply and collect the personalities, experiences and customs my future had designed for me. I shall be my own guide, determine where to go and whom to trust but also be susceptible to the unpredictability of fate. Fate may be what we claim as destiny; until I am exposed to Earth's bounty I cannot grow from its soil into a valuable human-being.

I've reflected on the arduous journey of my youth. Its completion would be the small fishing town of Collioure, half an hour by car, where I would eventually make my temporary home.

I had an address and a name and all the markings of

a foreigner, easy to pick out from a crowd: an apple in a box of pears. There were few passengers and no sign of a flustered French lady eager to clasp me to her bosom. It was then I realised my reaction was all wrong. I must take responsibility for my welfare, but first I needed to be collected, to find my feet in this new land, to use my ears and eyes and begin to learn.

Madame Simkin appeared, standing under the station clock: four o'clock in the afternoon. The arrivals filtered through like confused little fishes from nets. She resembled a modern-day Madonna, dressed in a brightly patterned cloak; a small hat framed her face which was thinly spread with a layer of white powder, eyes thick with black mascara and lips cherry-red. She was the cynosure of all eyes: brilliant and attractive, in the style and confidence of her age. Nearby Paul scratched his doggy back with a paw of long nails before arguing with a newspaper stand and chewing a loose printed corner, his pink tongue black with ink.

The French have neither *'th'* nor *'ch'* in their tongue. From day one Madame Simkin named me *'petit Paul'* after her dog. I was small for 16 years and I decided, without hesitation in this foreign climate, I would be pleased with my new selfdom. I enjoyed the policy of quick-conclusions and speedily I would learn to curb my sense of intolerance. After two minutes of meeting each other she tutted disdainfully at me through two fierce incisors and thrust her French accent into the tightening air between us, *'you is scroofy en smool; come petit Paul, mon doog. N'est pas?'*

Everything she ever said, compliments included -

for any association with her dog was a kind gesture of consideration - ended in a question. Her dog was a scrawny pale poodle with a torn ear; a confused runt who yapped at table legs. Madame was icy and awkward to melt, even with a little mustered English charm. *"Hello it's good to..."* the aposiopesis was numb. My words felt transparent, with an inability to administer any effect, unwilling to deliver the impact they were formed to make. My father's rule in the importance of first impressions, and those first few words I uttered, fell to the floor like feathers tied to lead.

Part II

Madame Simkin drove at hair-raising speed along the corniche into Collioure; bending and swerving and narrowly missing the rocky edges and sheer drop to the water below. She said she had *"a date in Banyuls."* It took my brain 10 minutes, a third of the journey's time to fully comprehend the one-sided conversation, some of which was directed to Paul; the name she had now bestowed upon me as well. Her accent was coarse, despite tipping my ear and lip-reading and following her excited gestures, I seldom fathomed much. I had to reconstruct the sentences. I told myself I would adjust to the rhythm and contours of her voice and when I'd learnt some real French speech, the comprehension would be clear and understandable. I actually quite liked her directness. She treated me like a capable young man and I would have to respond thus. At least she made an effort to speak in English, even her blasphemies made me hide a smile. This lady had *'a date!'* Naturally she did: a clutch bag, bangles, polished red leather shoes and a rose-perfume, all combined to announce her presence. She proffered a sound and scent before entering a room; she had style and elegance, and was keen to drop me off and begin her Friday evening.

The scenery was a beautiful expression of southern France. I could define cork trees and olive groves interspersed among the vineyards, planted roses and old pines, although this silhouetted outline does not do justice to a full vision of the landscape.

The first time I heard of Bette and Philly was on the slip road up to their house. Madame Simkin defined them as *"a kinde Erglish couple, amicable and gentile... juste marriaged."* With a grating of gears, she screeched to a halt outside a tall, narrow house, number 61. She knocked confidently on the dark-wood door of the pink-plastered building with blue shutters, a colour determined by the street lights. I will always remember being met by Philly's enthusiastic friendliness and Bette's radiance.

"Ah, good evening, hello, come in... Bette he's come, alright young man, give me your bag... your jacket... Thank you Madame... we'll take good care of him... Bette... he's come." Spoke Philly, full of charisma and gallant softness.

"I'm Philly, this is my wife Bette, and you are?"

"I'm Mothy, hello." I said cautiously and we shook hands.

"Mothy? Good of you to join us," Philly patted my back and took my suitcase, *"we've been waiting all week. Bette's been busy... here to learn some French... we're still trying, can't say we'll be much help."* Philly said jokingly. I watched Madame Simkin bite her lip and frown.

Bette, standing under the glow of a high lampshade, appeared to wear a halo. The light seemed to be drawn to her, or maybe she held her own luminosity. She was certainly attractive and well dressed.

"Hello Mothy... welcome... it's lovely to meet you."

Her hair was medium length and fair and she had a warm-brown complexion and penetrating, deep green eyes, they sparkled at me. She shone, I was exhausted, and I think I loved her.

Madame Simkin cried a reminder and farewell from her car, *"Classes begin Monday in Le Centre Culturel, à huit heures, n'est pas? You know Philippe!"* Already I was absorbing her French mixed with accentuated English. We waved her off and she was gone in a shot.

"She has a date in Banyuls," I said nonchalantly, then we all laughed and my nervousness dispelled. Philly couldn't stop chattering, and Bette gave me a hug. I think I must have fallen into her arms. I had not been hugged for a long while and at that moment I did not resist. As a public-school boy in the 1960s and with parents for whom physical affection did not come naturally, hugging was not part of my upbringing. I capitulated like a soldier taken. She knew me from the minute I stepped into their house; by nurturing me she would teach me to grow confident, to build strong roots and to enjoy being and developing myself.

After a simple hot meal together, one of Philly's stews, whereby he throws all sorts of vegetables and scraps into a pot, stirs in a tin of tomatoes and several generous pinches of dry herbs and marinates the contents on the hob for hours. The result was soft vegetables, the sauce burnt at the edges and chewy bits of something unknown. There was flavour and nourishment but most of all, and this is sometimes forgotten in cooking, there was time and kindness; the sense of giving regard and care to a soul full of appetite and wonder.

My bedroom was larger than expected, although, in truth, I did not know what to expect. Set against the wall was a single bed with two pillows, a small desk and chair with a side-light and a chest of drawers with a hand mirror and shoe brush, under the bed were additional empty boxes for storing paper, books and pens. The door had two pegs and a dressing gown hung from one; there was a small painting of a fishing boat bobbing on a sleepy bay, the sun rising or setting, I could not decipher which, and a couple watching the sky turn into hundreds of milky colours. The bedroom window looked down onto a courtyard with some small terracotta pots. Being at the top of the house I was able to survey the rooftops of the other cramped and tightly assembled houses. Behind this cluster of homes, the ear was led to the train line running along the base of a black and ruffled hillside and then the eye to an area of dense woodland and vineyards further beyond, here mountain and sky merged with one another.

"Fancy a crêpe, Mothy?" Philly shouted from the stairwell. *"They'll be open, I checked yesterday, start of the weekend everyone's open then."*

I made my way down carefully and he reduced his volume with each step.

"Nine o'clock's not very late over here, not like in England... kids stay up all hours and dine 'til late with their parents."

"Yes, thank you," I replied, *"what is a crêpe?"*

"Come and see, come on Belle, let's grab a rug and go!"

And so, we did. We walked as three: Philly then Bette and me, he called her Belle and stroked her hair, a light brown, interwoven with golden strands. She wore a necklace of pearls and pearl earrings, perched like rich drops of the moon on her ear lobes. Philly wore a checked shirt and jumper and small pair of glasses, they danced on his nose whenever he was animated. They danced all the time. On the edge of the town, before the little shops and bistros and bars began, was an open crêperie. The queue was eight people long which gave me time to decide what a crêpe was and what I wanted on it or in it or all over it. Young French children darted about and stared at me, whispered and ran off, then came back again and glared, smirked and ran off. If I'd been taller I would not have noticed their childish behaviour. However I was temporarily stuck at this height until I could grow and leave their little world behind. In age I was their superior, in height I was of equal stature. Perhaps I should eat more crêpes.

"What's it to be Mothy? Bette's having apple and calvados; I'm going for orange and Cointreau. Anything you like." Philly smiled at me.

"Um, chocolate?" I replied.

"Et un chocolat, s'il vous plait!" added Philly to the list.

A buxom woman nodded her head to the order. In front of her lay two large hot plates, she added a thumb of butter to each and began to pour a thin yellow liquid onto the hissing plates, one at a time with expert precision. She spread the batter with a small wooden rake until it dribbled over the side, then after a few seconds proceeded to upturn the fragile flaky pancake with a spatula, waving the utensil like Boudicca on her chariot, and began to layer and fill it with speed and delicacy. The finished crêpes were folded, the two alcoholic ones were set alight and burned for seconds, mine was covered in a rich, black sauce, hot and sweet. We each took our crêpes and I followed Philly and Bette to the beach; we sat on the rug, which Bette unfurled, and all took warm unabashed mouthfuls. No knife or fork. Bette had a method all of her own: slender and feminine. It felt almost rude to watch her. As an experience it was wonderful, as a snack it was sickly, but it was another excellent introduction to each other, a public display of messiness and abandoned inhibition.

"How d'you like it Mothy?" cried Philly.

"Oh! erm, nice."

"Oh, erm nice? We'll have to work on that!"

"Philly, leave him alone, it's been a long day... a long two days for Mothy. But your journey ends happily, as I felt, when I came here," Bette smiled slightly questioningly at Philly but he was too preoccupied, his neck craning to the heavens above, pointing and speculating.

We all gazed up at the October stars. How big the sky seemed across the sea, wide and deep and densely packed with mystery. I yawned, mesmerised by the ironic clarity of black. When there is less to look at, a vast black space of matter scattered with sparkling stars, there is more to explore inwardly. Your mind becomes the area of interest to colour a dark place. However, my extreme tiredness must have prevailed; the time from the beach until the next morning sits as an empty vacuum. It is without memory, an unfilled, uncoloured part of life, simply blank and obscure, age and time pass over, leaving no trace or explanation. This happens from time to time when recalling parts of the past.

Part III

Come morning as I struggled with my sleep-filled senses, my head attempted to place me. A delicate smell of yeast tingled around my nose, a slight suck of air frothed the scent. Bette worked a very early shift in the boulangerie two doors to the left. The bakers prepared the bread dough overnight, moulding, turning and resting it; they heated the wood-fire ovens, cut and shaped the naked dough then baked it brown. Sometimes they sprayed water into the piping ovens to create a hiss and a steam, making the crusts crack, split and spit like little waking monsters. They formed golden burnt edges and the flesh was soft, sour and sticky with occasional holes. When the loaves were made, Bette, with the lightest touch, set to work on the pastries; these required laminated doughs. A dough, folded with a rich unsalted butter, was set aside and she would make batches of *croissant au buerre, pain aux raisins*, the raisins mixed into a *crème anglaise* and twisted into snail-like rounds, commonly known as *escargots*. Her *pain au chocolat* were my favourite: two thick strands of bitter chocolate hidden inside a flaky, buttery pastry. Small *brioche* rolls and plaited *brioche* buns sprinkled with sugar crumbs also rose in the bakery. This was a flavour sensation, this was a French breakfast. A few of her own creations and any extra pastries, the ones caught by the oven, a little charred or chewy, or those handled too heavily (they had a rustic charm, but would not sell) with fruit, custard or chocolate seeping out the sides, were brought home. By 7am I was caught in an indulgent stupor. Battles

29

could be fought over the recipe of these more-ish morsels. Perhaps they would pacify aggression and unite factions if they were served, shared and enjoyed, in unanimous agreement, among opposing sides. How they would suspend tension and dilute angers!

Bette was not only beautiful, she dazzled me, with her tastes, quiet thoughts and her acts of affection. She encouraged me to tidy my belongings, organise my room and to *look as smart as possible,* for that first Saturday afternoon, we were making a visit.

At present, Philly was opening the local library, close to Le Centre Culturel, to a small group of mature students and would be back in the late afternoon. I was Bette's responsibility for the rest of the day. By 2pm I was washed and dressed and smelt somewhat oddly of sweet roses, the only soap I could find! Bette wore a cherry stamped neck scarf and matching skirt and jacket of brown wool; she declined my offer to carry her basket bag. I wanted to tell her how thankful I was to be staying with them, how kind and pleasant they were, and for making me feel so welcome. My mouth dried and my tongue, tied into knots, lay waiting to betray my words and mix my wishes into foolish mumbles. I smiled and asked plainly, *"where are we going?"*

She had a twinkle in her eye, one which seemed each time to enchant and captivate me. I heard my heart beat inside my inner ear, my blood quicken and flush my cheeks.

"I'll tell you on the way... it's just a short uphill walk to the

centre of town. I want you to meet Claudie."

On the narrow pavement, we walked side by side. I walked road-side. Although much smaller, I wanted to demonstrate my manners of protecting the lady from street traffic. I think she noted my intention. A few cars passed us; a light wind picked up and rustled the date palms and a white sailing boat circled the harbour. At this moment, I remember the scenery being of little importance, it was purely a backdrop to our characters. I was absorbed by Bette, and as I tried to calm my senses, her nature continued to fascinate me.

Claudie was a lady of 85 years. Bette had come to befriend her from early July. She herself had arrived in Collioure, *'at the end of June.'* I made a quick calculation in my head, Claudie would have been born in 1882. Bette was young to the Catalan region and of course newlywed to Philly. *'Juste marriaged,'* I could hear Madame Simkin's tone. Claudie had been born in Kent, *"the apple county."* I added. I was trying to show my intelligence, trying to bring myself closer to a story Bette owned. *"I'm originally from Warwickshire, William Shakespeare's county. We like to name our counties."* I scolded myself for stealing the air between us. From then on, I remained close-mouthed, I could hear the stern reverberations of my science teacher from the corner of my conscience, *'silence boys, those who listen, learn!'*

Claudie would surprise me. She lived in a small, but high-ceilinged room in her son's house. Tony worked full time at Port Vendres, for a shipping company. Bette came three afternoons each week to tend to Claudie's needs. She was slightly deaf in one ear, yet she was not in any way as dull or tedious, or as ordinary as you may assume. Claudie was capable of frying eggs, of reading novels and newspapers, of potting window boxes and bathing; what she lacked was stimulation, discussion and interaction. She longed to borrow ears, to tell tales of her youth. I was young and inexperienced. I was a blank canvas with an open mind and ready and willing ear. We were introduced and I was ushered onto a wicker chair with a cushion; the cushion hid a wide hole in the seat. Bette made three cups of tea each with a lump of sugar. The room was warm, Bette opened a window. She liked to open windows. She said *"it linked small worlds to bigger ones."* Claudie sat upright on her bed, stirred her tea with a finger, and cleared her throat, as if to prepare a trumpet for play. Bette smiled at me; she must have been watching my behaviour; the reactions running over my forehead like busy radio signals. I hoped she thought me a suitable companion.

Over the three-month period I lived in Collioure, Bette would take me to see Claudie on the Saturday afternoons I had available. Each time I would pull the wicker chair closer to her bed and listen to her distant tales of romance and romancing. I never knew how each affair of the heart began or how it ended. It was the flirtation, the allure of landscape, the idealization of love and the nostalgia of courtship she loved to portray. She had an impeccable eye for detail, each time she recalled her poetically-enhanced narratives, she, too, was painting a vivid picture of animated openness and colour.

There was the Italian buffalo farmer. She called him Prince Angelo; she believed him to have run away from royal responsibilities to live in the shadow of the Dolomites and *'feed on the milks of his homeland.'* They would ride *'rapidement'* down to the Venetian lagoon then wander into the damp churches of Venice, powdered by centuries of dust, listening to their own echoes of startled wonder, observing their stillness in awe.

There was the Parisian painter. She knew him as Francois, abandoned on the banks of the Seine. He was weaned by an elderly couple who passed away when he was 18, leaving him a ruined Chateau in Périgord with acres of ancient walnut trees, wild grasses and goat-herders. Occasionally they would stroll in the gardens of Versailles, picnic on *'une salade de fromages'* wrapped in wax paper and linen cloth and drink from the fountains of *l'Orangerie* to heal her chesty coughs.

The tale of Claudie's to follow, though sad, was my favourite. The day she told it was Bette's 31st birthday, Philly came too and we shared a gateau, made from cocoa and curls of rich chocolate, the best *le patissier* could boast.

"I arrived in Ronda, an ancient hilltop town in Andalucía, Southern Spain with a scrap of paper claiming the address of my father's sister, Helena. It was middle to late February; I can remember the day so clearly. My first impression of the old medieval town of Arab origin remains locked in my memory. I sat on a warm slab of stone close to the gorge watching black birds bend and dip in the secret currents of air that breathed below me; they hid in the crevices, disappearing and

reappearing between the great *Nuevo Puente*. It was called the New Bridge, the present structure having been completed in 1787. What a feat of engineering! I felt above the world, part of the sky, part of a kingdom, surveying the landscape that stretched to infinity. As far as the eye could see rolled a patchwork of greenery and as I directed my vision closer towards my position in Ronda, woods darkened the hills with their sweep of bushy trees. The farms, built of thick stone, managed healthy olive plantations and a steep hillside of almond blossoms brought the fresh pink blush of Spring.

Helena lived with her two small girls in a top floor apartment overlooking the great bullring in the El Mercadillo quarter. I distinctly remember a blue vase of bright yellow buds on the table. She told me 'it's mimosa, the lady's flower, the flower of the season.' The fluffy, pollen-laden flower-balls grow on a large bush or tree, have strong, waxy stems and a feathery, comb leaf.

After church one Sunday morning I was sitting with the girls beside a simple dark-stone fountain in the placa; Helena collected some sesame seed biscuit rings and a white loaf of bread for lunch. She'd hurried unnecessarily, and with great disappointment tore the edge of her long skirt. Helena cared enormously about looks and dress.

In the weak-burning winter light I caught a glimpse of a handsome young Spanish man. He was tall and slender with a small moustache and a sun-softened tan. He quickly turned to profile the minute I set my eyes on him, a sharp nose and long neck. He had, most definitely, spotted me already. His brown eyes had caught my face and his ears told him I was conversing in English with my two infantile cousins, now arguing over a strawberry bonbon, disrupting my serenity *with their pettiness. He was unfazed by my discomfort. He came over to me, so bold and assured, kissed my hand which melted into his palm and promptly invited me to walk with him that evening in the gardens, north of the bullring.*

For the next three weeks Antonio and I met every weekday night at 5pm, as the accordion player began his succession of canciones de amor. We walked for over an hour covering the sites and squares and hidden alleys of Ronda, crossing the bridge back and forth and stopping to admire breath-taking vistas. He climbed over a precipitous ledge to grasp a sprig of mimosa for my hair. The breadth of a weekend gave us time for trips to explore the orange and lemon groves of San Martín del Tesorillo. I have never tasted an orange so sweet. We cut them from the leafy trees, their zest burst a scent to my nose, honeyed and aromatic; we gorged on their syrupy juices, so much so my lips turned red. We climbed the white hill towns of Casares and Gaucín, wandered the sandy bays and beaches of the Mediterranean Sea, where I saw my first dolphin, and we rode two chestnut-coloured horses into the pine woods. Antonio worked on a horse ranch and was training to be a bullfighter; we spoke in broken Spanish and English. In Ronda, at every turn, there were more musical notes dressing the air: a harpist, a cellist, a Spanish guitar from an open window. On the last night, which I was not to know, he swept me into his arms and we danced just as the sun set and fell below the mountains, soothing the hard bricks and slippery, cobbled paths.

I returned to the bench every day until my own departure, a further three weeks later, he never came back to hold me. Two days before I was due to leave I was bathing the girls, a cumbersome task as they were perpetually squabbling over something or other, a letter arrived addressed plainly

'Claudie.' Of course it was from Antonio. His penmanship was very fine and he had a magnificent way with words, mixing the traditional easy English sounds with the vibrancy of Spanish; the whole mouth and body was used when reading his spirited mind and dexterity of hand. There was an apology, a line of poetry and the kind of conversation we had delighted in together. He also enclosed a small stem of mimosa, from his mother's garden, where he had been summoned for an indefinite length of time. The mimosa reminded him of me; the beauty of the spring after winter, the first splash of true colour, a flower which curls a smile and stirs a heart. He said 'mi mosa' meant my mosaic. He said, in our short time we were a mosaic, made up of so many different pieces... beautiful shades and shapes... something very special.

Helena forwarded his letters that followed to England each month with her own correspondence and the girls' pictures and messages. She did this for two years. Then she wrote to say, 'no letters have come.' Inside the envelope was a newspaper article, suffice to say a young bull-fighter, born to Ronda, had been killed instantly after a brutal attack in Seville. His name: Antonio Romo."

Bette's birthday almost became a day of mourning, she was so touched by Claudie's tale, she spent the rest of the afternoon constantly drying her weepy eyes and sniffing. There were so many questions she wanted answered, but then didn't want answered and when she raised her head in alignment with a question she shook it off. Until her dilemma was allowed to slowly simmer down, Philly and I were sent to buy some flour and eggs. On the way back we stood to throw some pebbles in the sea, a long distance from some swimmers, and to keep a silence because, as I learnt, a silence and a passing of time help salve the feelings of men.

When moods fell low or moments moved quietly, Philly always found conversation and consolation in the sky. A place, he felt, held so many mysteries. The stars, the planets, the moon, the solar system, the speculation of spaceships and other forms of life, the subjects were so vast, they rendered me dumb.

When the house was too small for three people plus the exceptionally grand set of emotions that came, living with two such unique individuals, I would take the opportunity to walk and talk with either one; we would freely disperse all debates and discourse to the sea and sky.

"There's something magical out there... can't explain it well, but I feel it. I'm a far-fetched believer Mothy! If there is such a thing!" Philly looked left to right, checking his proximity to others. He pointed a hand to the sky as if to introduce another member to our party of two. The light was fading, drifting into early evening pinks, a sharp flash of colour before the sun made its rapid descent below the horizon.

Philly spoke with a keen composure. *"New places to explore... why humans have already gone into space from Earth! There may well be another Earth out there, with their science and civilisation ready and waiting to visit us. I'm not satisfied in believing we're the only planet of a highly-developed race. It's a fanciful notion Mothy, I know."* Philly sighed. *"We might be a sleepy town in Collioure, not so connected to the big cities or some such university, but the* beauty of nature and space is far more visible here than in labs and study rooms."

He continued on an exhausted breath, "Staring at books and blackboards is important, but my blackboard is the sky, every time I look up I hope to understand more."

"When you read books," he nodded towards me, "you dive deep into the words or the tale and read something that increases your learning... it alters your head and re-positions your ideas... you're taught by novel or by poem or by book. The sky we must try to read without words... it's one big picture puzzle. Even if we have to follow the stars and join them dot to dot."

I could not make any sensible additions to Philly's imaginings, I followed his outpourings and his humour. It felt good to be out in the open air, fresh from a day's warmth; the autumnal scent of smoked chestnuts and the timeless turn of seawater washing and sculpting the rocks.

"When I look to the sky and stars, I realise how small we are and how immense the universe is... all our day to day problems and issues just fizzle out when you consider the cosmos far, far above us... a system still so untapped and inexplicable. You'll have to tolerate my whimsical ways! I'm not a public speaker just a passionate Earthly thinker." Philly let these opinions stew in the air before switching back, as if he had changed the channel inside himself.

"Let's go home to Bette, she'll be wondering about us. We need to put a smile on her face."

Part IV

This was to be a three-month course of immersion into the language and the life of France. For the sake of my sanity and yours, I will not describe the lessons in the detail I was forced to endure them, however, they were the basis of my stay. Even then and with a touch of hindsight I knew this visit would mean more to me than solely lessons in French. This was the beginning of a new phase, of forming and shaping new ideas, of discovering new worlds, facing challenges and fears and finding friends, foes and myself. Over and over again in the years of building life, the principles apply. This start, in the town of Collioure. would always stay as my longest running memory.

The first Monday of lessons was the hardest to face. Madame Simkin brought her discontented personality to the classroom and her face of ready-dissatisfaction. Paul, on the other hand, lay comfortable-in-the-extreme on a rug in a corner basket with an array of potential distractions: a tired ball, stick of bleached driftwood from the beach and a few crunchy dog biscuits.

A small group of nervous looking pupils began to assemble inside Le Centre Culturel. Philly stood beside me and encouraged us all to introduce ourselves while a distracted Madame Simkin gathered her papers and *livres d'etudiants.* She kept a red pen hidden in her bouffant hairstyle, when she reached for the slippery *stilo*, which she lost many-a-time, placing it behind an ear or up a sleeve, it was a sign of error and correction.

Hannah, a co-student, was a broad-shouldered girl with fly-away brown hair. She was tall for sixteen and clearly still adjusting to her growth-spurts, although she knew how to use them to distract or ignore. Flicking her hair from front to back was both a sign of *'look at me'* and *'I'm not interested in having anything to do with you.'* She was a dominant, looming and robust figure, capable of adult flirtations and an out-pouring of adolescent tears.

Louis and Michael were brothers from Surrey, with only 18 months between them. Louis was the more engaging and I expected him to be the eldest, but that was Michael, the shy, studious and helpful brother. Madame Simkin assumed with the French name Louis, he would naturally grasp the language. She liked the texture of its sound on her lips and called him up to read in class twice as many times as the rest of us. Louis had, quite candidly, joined his brother in lessons abroad to escape the monotony of lessons at home.

Carolyn, who very quickly became Lyn, was friendly and conscientious. She was half Irish and very charming. Her rhythmic Irish lilt, her urge to chatter and to display the activeness of her mind were great assets in commanding the tricky accent of the Roussillon dialect. I found the articulation extremely trying in speech and in listening. It was Lyn who encouraged me not to form such perfect, coherent sentences, these were correct in theory but speech gave more latitude for experimenting. My written work was well-approved, orally the sentences required flavour. My pronunciation was too ordinary; I had to roughen the cadence of my voice and develop the hard-foreign tonality. A coarse and unrefined accent coupled with gesticulation and body language would help to lift my dialogue. Lyn gave invaluable advice and, in practise with Bette, I was able to progress. All influences of learning are not necessarily found in class. Life is directed and challenged by guidance.

Lyn blended well with boys and girls of all ages and even managed to make Hannah laugh with her flamboyance and daring sense of fun. She had grown up as one of 8 children and understood what it was like to fight for your character, to mix your personality among a throng of energetic, loud and boisterous siblings. She claimed to be the quieter and more obliging child of the family. She held your eye with such penetration, she could predict your next word and, causing some annoyance, liked to finish sentences. She was seldom without people around her, and always the one on whom attention was laid.

There was Edward, a boy of 16 and, judging by a school badge and uniform jumper, my type. He was so happy to be in Collioure. However, I decided this joy stemmed more from a sadness he left behind than the present challenge of French classes. I later learned his mother had suffered a breakdown and his father drank himself into an oblivion so wretched he did not even recognise his own son returning home for the holidays.

Finally, two sisters, Imogen, known as Gen and Jennifer, known as Jenny. Gen was the protective sister, strong-minded yet pleasant with a melodramatic energy. She and Lyn occasionally clashed outside lessons, this was merely to do with the fact they were so doggedly similar in thought. Should chance arise, incidentally, in which they were diametrically opposed in opinion, an angry silence would ensue until the matter passed over, each concluding they had won. It was with thanks and reluctance I understood how complicated girls could be and how really young men are relatively simple and straightforward.

Jenny was very pretty. She had rosebud lips, a few freckles and a smile that curled along the left side of her face. She kept close by her sister and admired Gen's self-assurance, for what Jenny lacked in confidence, she made up for in beauty. This somehow made her lovelier, for not fully understanding the impact of her looks gave her a balance and harmony; she was angelic, modest and not suited to the irksomeness of instruction.

To be brief, yet thorough, as this is not the true object of my writing, lessons were Monday to Friday. Beginning at 8.30am, the mornings were written and listening work: improving vocabulary, vernacular, and conjugating verbs. The midday break period was two hours, each student returned home to their host for lunch and short rest before returning for afternoon sessions. Madame Simkin encouraged us each to participate, to think, and to act in French. By the afternoon, we would concentrate on conversation and interaction, sometimes in twos or as a group; ask questions and raise any queries or points of interest.

One day Madame Simkin decided to teach us a few French idioms: *'expressions idiomatiques.'* It was the final lesson, late on a Friday and she was in a particularly jovial and mischievous mood; she appeared to revel in the strangeness of language. I also had my suspicion she must be entertaining her 3rd date of Banyuls. The two idioms I have considered and that resonate over the course of my life will always remind me of a class full of laughter. Firstly, there was *'donner sa langue au chat,'* - *'to give one's tongue to the cat,'* - *to give up.* Any mention of *'chat'* made Paul bark sharply, his ears prick excitedly and his tail wag uncontrollably. There was a moral to it as well and she made sure we understood. Idioms were created not only as amusements, there were always delightful messages contained within them. In this case we were *not* to give up but to work through an obstacle patiently. They were memorable and quirky short sentences, individual and unique, like ourselves.

Secondly, there was *'pedaler dans la semoule' – 'to pedal in the semolina' – to go around in circles.* Madame Simkin rolled the phrase off her tongue with fluent irony. After the hilarity of discussing the peculiarities of language in class and finding an idiom best-suited to each one of us, I clearly recall asking Bette and Philly for their favourite idioms. Philly had replied, with a flash-back of regret and coolness, *"O the worn-out phrase, 'to have bitten off more than you can chew.'"* He spoke as if he had suffered the impact of the words more than once. *"Wasn't as smart as I thought I was, there was always someone else much brighter than me. They knew more, true, but I had a passion, a feeling for things, beyond theory."*

Bette smiled. For her it had to be, *"oh, 'over the moon,' like when I met Philly!"* Philly kissed her cheek to cheek. Her testimony caused no embarrassment; they were so liberal and affectionate to one another. The formal, static and repressed ways of English love seemed attached to old plays, devoted to poetry or entrenched in novels.

At the end of each week we endured a spelling and grammar test and occasionally a talk from a local Collioure inhabitant. By the middle of October, Simone, a young woman, came to discuss, in French, her small restaurant business in town with a sea-view of the safe bay. She described the interior, the menu and her daily work and habits. Madame Simkin nodded approvingly. The aim of the presentation, as Madame recognised it, was to enlighten our minds, to improve listening, understanding, interpretation, composition and to garner new words and phraseology. At the end of her talk when all the students, bar myself, had left, the noise and hubbub fell to silence and the air refilled, Simone began a brief conversation with me.

She was a friend of Bette's, they had travelled together to Collioure in June. While Bette had taken work at the boulangerie, Simone had taken over the running of the little restaurant, now known as Chez Simone, from a recently widowed man. It seems he, Frank, had come over in 1948, three years after the end of the Second World War, determined to help this poor and fractured area of Vichy France. Wounded and embittered, he sought, along with other proprietors, to rebuild the pride and honesty of the good-natured but battered people. After his return to his homeland, Simone was now running, and slowly prospering, the difficult business with a committed team of local *'personnel.'*

Simone was of similar stature to Bette. She held the style of a young French lady, with the attention to detail of frock, hair and accoutrements. Hanging elegantly on a loose snake-chain was a small deep blue jewel, shiny as if freshly varnished, it resembled a piece of the sky. Yes, indeed, if you were to cut a tiny piece of *'cielo'* on a clear summer's day, this would be its beautiful illustration. Bette had a jewel of similar likeness, above the fireplace, she cared for it like an icon. It was sacred to her, an incarnation or embodiment of something far greater than its little self.

Simone and Bette had not contacted one another of late and she encouraged us, on hearing I had joined Bette and Philly, to come visit, *"au weekend... l'hiver est calme, donc je suis ouvert juste les week-ends."*

Madame Simkin detested the Anglicisation of words she would have tutted, her vocal trademark of displeasure, *'Non, pas le week-end! C'est la fin de la semaine.'*

Simone left in a hurry, as did I, my head in a disordered whirl. Walking from Le Centre Culturel to home I would rewind my hours and process everything. The clouds, churned and pulled by a high air current, were stretched across the sky, thin and white and all manner of shapes. Philly's tendency to look up and into the skies was becoming a habit of my own; reading the contours of a twisted cloud; applauding the first bright star to shine through at early evening; admiring the tinge of pink stream under the belly of a fluffy cloud floating tentatively on the hillside before dissolving as quickly as it was created, into the heavens.

By the time I walked through the door the aroma of sautéed shallots would engulf me, with dear Bette, in the front room, opening a window and Philly in the kitchen struggling with a frying pan and cutlery, yelling unconvincingly, *"everything's under control!"* At once, and with joy, my thoughts were pulled into the moment, I had drifted home on a breeze.

Part V

In Collioure market day hours fall after church on Sunday. It was customary for each town, however small, to hold a market at least once a week and on different days so that one could, if inclined, visit a market every morning of the week, every week of the year, with the exception of religious holidays. The market enlivened the darker squares and corners of the town, and many, if not all, of the shops and family-run cafés and bars were open and bustling. Visitors, meandering the short stroll downhill from the train station, came armed with empty bags. Often a poodle was harboured in one, or when the bag no longer afforded refuge but instead stored aromatic leeks, the peevish pet settled in the capacious area under its owner's arm. The market was more than shopping it was a whole way of living. It was the epicentre of all aspects of life: food, music and gossip tantalised every one of the senses. It was the heart of society: the breath of being and the sight of seeing.

The food section was a spectacle, a true goblin market of temptations. Bette carried two large bags and wandered from stall to stall. I followed her and Philly walked behind with a dedicated interest. There was some lively music playing. To begin with I could not locate its source, so I made a guess at the instruments: an accordion, a guitar, a bass. The acute concentration I applied to listening in class was proving convenient in its application to other aspects of life! By paying close attention, one could go on to interpret situations with greater insight and to translate the world in a more intuitive way; to see it not only as it appears to oneself but how it is used, embraced and studied by others. The examination of words and sounds heightened the consideration and contemplation of people and their actions.

The small band, now accompanied by a lady vocalist, had placed themselves neatly on a corner just outside the market square. Browsing, with spirited music, *"makes you stay longer and spend more,"* said Philly to my ear. He was tapping his feet and humming and whistling, then added, *"I feel young and free and happy to be here!"*

Bette encouraged me to speak French, deal with the cost and sums and hand over the francs. Much of the produce came from garden allotments, grubby with soil and from nearby farms or vineyards. In October we were selecting black figs, small and fat, *"edible mini-spaceships"* Philly described them. Two or three were split to reveal a pink tangle of seeds and oozing sticky syrup. To Philly, everything was not only itself, it always bore a resemblance to something else. Some of the more bruised and scorched figs were being boiled into *confiture,* bobbing and spitting in a hot preserving pan. There were sweet bunches of Muscat grapes, *"the fruit of the Gods... perfect for pinching from the table, as you never can tell how many have been eaten."* Then we weighed three long, red peppers, *"the white seeds were elf coins,"* gathered a bundle of pungent leeks, a handful of haricot verts, *"pixie fingers,"* several smooth and glistening aubergine, *"fairy pillows,"* some dirty, knobbly potatoes, *"moon bricks,"* a bunch of flat-leaf parsley, *"dragon's hair,"* Philly went on, until Bette gave him one of her penetrating feminine glares, and before Philly could make one last quip, Bette picked a bulb of pink garlic, *"to keep the aliens at bay!"* she beamed. Her eyes twinkled, Philly and I were caught by her sparkle. To me she made a remarkable impression: she seized the eye, she heated my pulse and revived my energies.

Philly suggested I savour some of the cheeses on display. Three different stages of goat's cheese, from fresh and lemony to a mouldy rind, we took both, then a slice of firm, buttery *'tomme'* and a blue-veined round. While Philly was sampling a third variation of brie, I spotted Bette chatting vigorously with Simone and felt a sudden pang of guilt for not having forwarded the message to visit her restaurant. From the look on their faces and the occasional flair of animated sound, they were taking time for a fair reunion. I lingered, caught sight of Hannah who was discreetly smoking a cigarette under one of the plane trees. There were roughly twenty, full-leaf trees to frame the market square. I glimpsed Edward and Lyn sharing a crêpe. I left my observations alone and the two to themselves and returned to my own family.

When the *paniers* were full to bursting, Bette handed the contents to Philly. She then enjoyed the benefits of free hands to scoop and choose some ripe *'tomates anciennes.'* The heritage tomato requires a story all of its own, with its slender ridges, patterned stripes and rainbow skin, the taste and texture is unsurpassable. Philly agreed there must be a fable attached to this fabulous fruit. Bette ensured Philly and I had one most days - sprinkled with sea salt and olive oil or eaten with the same informality as an apple. The final purchase was a loaf of bread. The market provided a large stall of more specialised breads than the traditional boulangerie staples. During the week villagers patronised their local bakers. All the breads were made of white wheat flour, water, yeast and salt then moulded into a variety of forms: *fougasse, epi, campagnette, boule.* Essentially all of the same dough, but crafted into a selection of individual shapes, each of which I came to know and subsequently became as assertive and as emphatic as any Frenchman. The buyer would choose a loaf most befitting their meal of the day, usually midday when the *clocher* frantically alerts daily life with its twelve insistent strikes. How much of French life is focused on food, the pleasure and consumption of it! On this particular Sunday Bette had ordered a round *pain aux noix,* one of the more expensive loaves. She wanted me to experience the cleverness of such a creation: toasted creamy walnuts and a wholesome crust, a perfect accompaniment to the cheeses and salads. We repeated this process together every Sunday I was in Collioure. Sunday became the day I looked forward to the most. I would feel the agitation rise and the thrill of expectancy, the heightening of senses and the absolute conviction, there was nowhere else like this in the world.

The following Thursday had been a frustrating day of learning. Madame Simkin was increasingly malcontent, distracted by Paul's incessant scratching and whimpering, a new technique he had perfected for ensuring attention. Everything vexed her, the unseasonably mild weather or the pattern of her *foulard;* she refused to budge from her exceptionally dissatisfied conduct. She was volcanic. Sadly she erupted at me for my grammatical faults; her make-up appeared to move independently from her features, a few seconds behind her aggravation. Then she scolded Louis; a perplexed expression crossed her face, *why does this French-named child not speak like a child of France?'* At the close of class, everyone had been sternly rebuked for something. Poor Jenny whose smallest error of *'la chat'* instead of *'le chat'* had seemed the gravest, primarily because it was the simplest. Once again it provoked a reaction from Paul, despite the preposition being so terribly wrong. Inexcusable. Perhaps Madame's Friday date had been postponed, or cancelled or worse still, maybe it was the end of the Banyuls affair.

Luckily, Bette had suggested collecting me after school for a *'racione'* at *Chez Simone.* I was not sure of the word, and to save my embarrassment Bette explained the meaning: a small plate of simple delicious food, slightly larger than *tapas.* Time for some food education as the previous week I had agreed to try Philly's version of *poulpe* stew, believing it to be chicken. The obvious error had come about as I had observed the spelling on a shopping list he had forgotten to take to work, *poulet* being the French word for chicken. I had had a violent reaction to *poulpe* (octopus), taken the day-off school, (my first and only) and, was quite happily and gently, nursed back to health by Bette's wisdom. She infused dried camomile with hot water followed by another hot concoction of a slice of lemon and freshly rubbed mint, grown in the tubs.

Simone was polishing wine glasses and folding napkins when we arrived. Jacques her principal waiter and

Marcel, her portly, fastidious chef, were lifting tables onto the raised stone path at the front, overlooking the church and beach. The restaurant was empty of customers, 5pm was an ideal time for quiet company. It was too late to say, *'bonjour'* and it was too early for *'bonsoir'* so I came forward and offered a *'bon apres-midi'* into the empty margin between us.

"Bon apres-midi et bienvenue à *Chez Simone,"* flushed Simone. *"Prenez une table et je viens tout de suite."*

Jacques winked at Bette and we took the table he had just laid, with a little blackboard menu placed upright offering *'plats du jour.'* Bette did not respond to the wink, which she might have missed, and quite suddenly I felt defensive. She was Philly's wife, what would Philly say? He'd say, *"this is France my lad, better out for all to see it, than in and all to guess at!"*

Simone brought over two glasses of Muscat, the drink with the flavour of sunshine. She also brought a jug of fresh lemon water and a dish of golden, Catalan almonds: toasted ovals, ridged on the surface and consumed in two smooth bites. The late afternoon sun shone bright on the bricks, drawing out the warm pastel colours of the seafront houses and casting long linear shadows of the moving objects: the *promenader* and his poodle. Bette and Simone chattered on all topics of conversation in a splattering of English and French: the weather, the restaurant, the food and the people. Privately I detected my own pull towards the impressions of the sky. It was innocently blue with a thin spread of ruffled white, *'the white hairs of a brush pulled across blue.'* Philly could write a narrative for every aspect of sky. I thought, in this region of fair France, *'how could you look at the great expanse above and not wonder at its possibilities?'*

Philly's influence and the magnetism of Bette, made me question and observe this new unparalleled life into which I was becoming immersed.

Simone and Bette shared a plate of grilled local anchovies dusted with parsley and a wedge of lemon, and a mixture of roasted *legumes*. They blushed with mingled pleasure.

My reputation for a light stomach, surpassed my desire to experiment with new foods. Jacques delivered a small plate of toasted baguette rubbed with tomato, *"pan con tomate, bon appetit!"* he demonstrated his half Spanish, half French intelligence bordering on irony with the smuggest of smiles. I attempted to see past his sarcasm, if he realised his attitude had no effect on me, that I could not be riled, he would have to give up. Consequently, he continued to treat me as the little boy at the table, ensuring I had a napkin to wipe my oil-stained hands and when I was awkwardly angling tomato and bread towards my mouth, he chose the very moment to say, *"c'est bon, n'est pas?"* Finally he withdrew to the kitchen on receiving a stern stare from Simone. He emerged again to welcome some clients to the tables inside and when we left, some two hours later, he emitted a polite, *"au revoir Bette et Mothy."* I was surprised he'd remembered my name, he had taken little notice of my introduction, perhaps Simone had noticed his slight contrariness or the derision quivering over his every word and manner toward me.

I concluded both Bette and Simone, two women of similar humour, had the ability to work magic over men, whether it be in word or in wonder.

By early evening there was a warm whisper of wind, scented with pinecone oil. Swallows chased across the sky, dipping to feed on dozy flies, then twisting and curling their bodies like paper-planes, anticipating the Saharan winds ready to send southern signs of a more favourable climate. The starlings, in their murmuration, were beginning to dance and startle, flocking together in their hundreds to roost in trees of a rustling, sibilant sound. Finally, most distinctive of all yet untraceable in his hiding, was the melody of a songbird. In England, it would be a garden warbler with his chorus of rippling water notes and of bubbles, imitating a meandering stream, swallowing the joys of both the river's song and its water. The scene, which Bette and I took a moment to absorb, was tranquil, a time of in-betweens, neither day or night. A time when thoughts relax and the goodness and beauty of nature rests on the conscience. The song of a single bird, the dissolving of colours into the sky, the breadth of landscape and curl of sea penetrate the affections and with all naturalness abide thereafter, sleeping in the memory.

Overnight there was a sudden cascade of rain, the gods casting about their untidy grief. The torrent washed clean the tiled rooves, drenched the wispy, blue plumbago bushes and tumbled along the gutters and river-alleys to refill the sea's purse.

Part VI

On the third Saturday of November, falling on the 18th I found myself alone for the first time in six weeks. Having been so accustomed to company and attention, the atmosphere was dull; the day outdoors an undecided assortment of colour. I would have to seek entertainment of my own. Edward and Lyn had, mid-week, invited me for a crêpe. I had refused, perhaps too quickly, for the look on Lyn's face showed an element of reflectional rudeness. Edward feigned his sorrow, he enjoyed having Lyn's unrivalled attention; she appeared to enjoy an *ensemble* of people, a crowd on whom she might gregariously practise and perform her Irish wit and humour, a technique she was now developing in French.

For me, the weekends revolved around Bette and Philly's plans. On this day, however, the house was empty with a few tell-tale signs of life before 9am: a small fire burning in the front-room, plumped cushions on the armchairs, some clean washing, which I dispersed. Philly had boxed some old books and clothes for the loft; in the kitchen lay a little breakfast plate of two mini pain au chocolat and a helping of jam and fruit, and a note: *'Dear Mothy, I'll be home no later than six, Philly's at Le Centre Culturel, comme d'habitude! À bientot, Bette x'*

Bette kept a diary, tucked into her handbag. Each week she wrote a postcard to a friend or acquaintance, she loved to write and describe everything, she told me. Occasionally she'd sketch a *vignette,* a small scene, mostly outside, weather permitting, finding a quiet and sheltered spot to illustrate a small, graceful view. One or two of her latest images were on the mantel-piece; a small part of the house she held for herself. Philly had the loft space. Instinctively we all find sections of home that are more our own than anyone else's and we can have complete design over their use. In fact, they are a small extension of ourselves. Nico used our toy-room to complete jigsaw puzzles and build mini sky-scrapers, he became an architect, and I made use of our small tree-house, restoring and designing the interior with salvaged home pieces, wallpaper and spare carpet. In the holidays, I was to be found bird-watching, reading adventure stories and scribbling my own ambitions. I would spend whole days, whether warm or wet, actively entertaining myself, obediently returning to the kitchen when called. I would make an occasional familial appearance at a function so as to prevent any curious intrusion or alarm and then disappear again.

Bette told me the loft, the last time she ventured up there, was as scatty as Philly, full of disordered hobbies and interests he couldn't decide upon. She made no mention of her spaces, they were always neat and polished with a collection of curious nature-table attractions.

I decided to go searching for Bette. Were we not meeting to visit Claudie? Did she expect me by now to have traded my afternoons at her side in favour of a snack and an unexciting walk with my week-long companions?

I could not disturb Philly and his festival work. Philly was at his most fretful when he was preparing the local festivities. Admittedly the season for outdoor celebrations was drawing to a close. He employed these simpler, less demanding days by keeping indoors, judging posters for next year's saints' days or sorting and mending tatty library books. Last week he had brought home a small sample of three locally grown and blended, new season wines. In early summer, he worked in cultivating the olives on the steeped, dry-stone walls of the Museum's olive grove. He had a fondness for the ancient olive trees, as old as the Bible, with their flaking paper-thin bark and bitter, emerald-green oval fruit or the nicoise, a juicy jet black. The gnarled and twisted trunks revealed a smooth, silky wood of blended browns. Philly collected some dead branches to turn on a lathe he kept in the attic. He was a novice, self-taught and seldom turning, but it was the thought he might one day turn and create something worth displaying that kept him keenly gathering. The younger specimens of the grove were straight with delicate, silvery-green leaves that whispered when the winds passed through them, *'musical trees with magical fruits,'* Philly had once said. Being amongst the purity of nature gave him clear vision, the sea gave him solace and the sky, mystery.

He organised the blessing of the fishermen and fish for a successful harvest of the sea and the August glorification of St Vincent. To his mind, however, the most poignant ceremony was the annual honouring of the dead at the War Memorial in the Old Town square. The short solemn service had taken place the previous week.

I was keen and quick, walking uphill into town, taking the longer route, allowing myself time to think like Bette. Had she taken these steps? Where might I find her? The first thought to spring to mind was obvious, with Claudie, so I headed there without the weight of a second thought, lest it slow my pace.

"*Non*," said a grumpy Tony. I'd disturbed his eating hour, an unfortunate crumb loosely stuck to his hairy chin. He chewed his language with a gruff voice and flaunted a shrug of the shoulders.

"*She'll be 'ere... l'apres-midi, normalment à deux heures. Viens et tu peux attendre en haut.*" (*normally at two o'clock in the afternoon. Come in and you can wait upstairs*). He opened the door wide on its hinges.

Tony associated me with Bette, so engaged a little more than most would expect. He was the epitome of the earthy, rugged Southerner. He owned a proud, tobacco-stained beard, a high sun-browned forehead and dry, blistered lips. He was tall and brawny, with a head hung low, possibly from continuous talking to fellows below him and from exercising his work in a low-slung habit. His hands were swollen and sore and his shirt splashed with spots of a deep-red wine. He was Claudie's son and I wanted to like him. I was daunted by his stature; he lacked manners but his manliness was more than evident. I felt the flood of intimidation run through my veins. I was charged with heat and anxiety. There was I, inwardly growing a sense of maturity, only outwardly still very much fitting my 16-year-old shoes, rudely disturbing the homely comforts of this hard-working *monsieur*.

I heard a voice above and darted upstairs. Claudie, in a long, warm woollen dress and apron, with her back to me and her thoughts and song to the window, was drying a plate and fork. I brushed my rumpled trousers and jumper; my jittery turn had resulted in an unkempt, mis-matched collection of clothing.

"Sorry to disturb you Claudie, I was looking for Bette, I thought she might be here. Pardon, je ne voulais pas te deranger." I fumbled.

"Entrez, entrez, asseyez-vous." Claudie pointed to the usual guest chair with the cushion. Both her English and French were clear and faultless.

"Ah, Non!" She changed her mind, patted another sturdier chair, indicating I might remove the pile of heavy books and sit upon it more comfortably. This I did with consideration. There was a photo album, lying on top. She gestured I should look through it. Odd, sepia photos glued to black card, a history in pictures of her family long gone: loved and lost. The characters and personalities of her tales.

"How do you like it 'ere Mothy, settled at last?"

"Oh, lots, I've been here six weeks now," I said

"Mais oui! Six semaines déjà!" She chattered to herself.

"Don't worry about Tony," she stamped her slipper quietly, *"He's not charmant, but his heart is good. When Bette comes, he'll make an effort otherwise he's a bit of a disgruntled 'ours,' you know 'ours?' A bear!"*

"Oh, I knocked at the wrong time... I was thinking about Bette's routine, I see I'm too early."

Claudie settled onto her bed and wrapped a shawl around her shoulders, she declined any offer of help. *"Si tu m'aides, tu ne m'aides pas,"* (if you help me, you don't help me). Her sharpness and stubbornness was part of her personal dignity; she used her age as an advantage to be sometimes brusque but well-meant. Bette had warned me and reminded me on occasion, to find no harm or malice in her gruff or short remarks, age gave her entitlement, to some extent. I was certainly too young to build resentment or dislike in one always so riveting in speech and replete in wisdom. Why she was a contemporary of Virginia Woolf and James Joyce!

Claudie began with no encouragement, like any narrator she simply jumped outright into conversation as easily as a child.

"Bette's an unusual woman, unlike any I've known... and I've been around a while. She met Tony in the market, early July, it was... both of them picking out a punnet of raspberries, or maybe les strawberries, I forget."

"Bette does like confiture de framboises." I added.

"Very well, let's say raspberries. As sweet as the ones I remember from Kent farms. Sometimes we'd go foraging. Then one day I was caught scrumping. For punishment, I was to spend all the summer months collecting and selling the berry. Some as compotes, some as pies, jams, preserves... every which way, we strove to conserve them. They were a real luxury... the cost was high and for many northern markets far

too expensive. I lost my taste for them for years after... until we moved to Collioure... it's been over 60 years!"

She glanced at the weather outside. *"Clouds coming in off the sea, maybe rain later, unless the winds blow them back, then the rain showers fall over the horizon in grey smudges. Many times I've seen the odd cloud get stuck on the hillside and deposit its belly full of rain on the vineyards. The wine-growers welcome it. They call it Bacchus."*

She paused, a short unbroken silence and a glance at my face must have spelled my interest in Bette.

"Oh, Tony mentioned he'd never seen anyone quite like Bette. Her kind eyes, softly spoken voice... ears that genuinely listened and learned... just what he wanted for me." Claudie cleared her throat.

"The following week she came to meet me and has joined me in tea and conversation ever since... just as you do."

Her tone changed. *"Do you want a drink?"* I shook my head and returned the offer, she declined and continued, *"I'm sorry if I upset her birthday. I have, through age, grown a more selfish heart. I was a young, travelling romantic once upon a time... I should have known she's just the same."*

"Do you know much about Philly?" I asked.

"Philly? Non, nothing at all, only what Bette tells me. He was much quieter than I expected when you all came over, but I understand that. Good friends, even on another's territory, are often more shy versions of themselves. The first time I

met Bette she said Philly had rescued her soul, soon after she'd arrived in Collioure... or some such. They met at Les Templiers. What was it she said?" Claudie looked to me and frowned and then to the window and relaxed her face.

"I remember it now, it was a beautiful line she composed, 'he captured my heart with his enthusiastic interests, he rescued my soul with his curious words; he never questioned my spirit or individuality; I held his concentration and he held mine. I knew he'd be honest and faithful.' She said she'd be happy with 'his mix of gentle simplicity, curiosity and his unending questions on the marvellous and spectacular.' Why Bette has a remarkable inner self, it's untapped and unknown to most, I bet even Philly doesn't know half of what Bette could tell him. She seems happy to let him be the shining star."

"What do you know of Bette?" I asked.

Claudie needed little prompting. *"Bette has an undimmable sparkle. I know she's come a long distance. Collioure seems to be a place of converging magic, of invisible energies, of boundless creation and inspiration and inexplicable magnetism, all of it positive, whether founded in the Earth, the Sky or the Sea. I've always followed the yearnings of my heart... when I arrived here, I knew I could stop searching."*

How wise and thoughtful was Claudie. She would have been Bette's age when the Great War broke; not one of her romances ever touched upon those four Earth-shattering years. Nor did she bring into conversation any of her experience of the world's second foray into the slaughter of War. A time, so horrendous in reality, was to be hidden and refused the air of open discussion. She had lived an extraordinary life, a life valued at more than one person. She was perceptive and astute, conjuring emotional and physical prophesies, like an otherworldly genius.

After two hours with Claudie and no sign of Bette, it was agreed I would leave her to sleep and to dream. Spending time with Claudie, her stories and observations, was a tiring process for her, and to utter informally, eye-opening for myself. Firstly, her tales required concentration and were sourced from a deep, idealistic inner eye: the mind's eye. She had to search the far corners of her memory to retrieve these dramas, then elaborate, nourish and present them with eloquence and respect, as if they had occurred only last week. Any lady who had lived and loved as she had would want to seize and hold on to the elegance of life.

On walking home I took the flat route around the perimeter of the 17th century castle. Sandwiched between the safe beaches, the Kings of Mallorca Castle dominates the seafront with its long, steeply-sided and fortified sandy-stone walls. The cupola look-out posts and the sharp-pointed edges are defensive architectural enhancements by the great military engineer Vauban. It's a foreboding and imposing structure, being so grand and impenetrable. The interior of the castle was a maze of rooms and uneven alleys, at Madame Simkin's command we had taken a guided tour.

I stopped to gaze at the castle façade and wondered

how Claudie might perceive me. What would she say of me to Bette or Philly or Tony (about whom I was less concerned)? How did I appear? For it is certain we are all viewed and recognised differently by different people, depending on our relationship to them as well as many other factors such as age or location. Did I portray the person I judged myself to be? Was I understood as I wanted to be? Were any of us? Bette for one. As people of Earth, we can only do our best. Others, wishing to think and know more, will fill the gaps with their own presumptions, predictions or speculations.

When the castle basked in sunlight, even in the short, pale, winter sun, the honey-coloured stone looked as soft as a sand-castle. When tides were whipped high, the sea wall protected the bay from the violent impact of wild and destructive storms. Against the castle border and walk-way, the sea-water flowed coaxingly and shallowly, and on these days access was impassable. I kept moving. Saturday couples and crowds were strolling leisurely; I nipped in and out of their wake. Beyond the immediate flurry, I caught sight of a low-lying cloud nestling in the hillside, fastening other little clouds to its waist, growing fleshy, heavy and pearly. 'Bacchus' I thought. Maybe Claudie, with age and sagacity, really could look at the world and interpret more than the naked eye can see and the human ear can hear.

I briefly joined Edward and Lyn, who had feasted on unenviable crêpes and were feeling queasy. I actually enjoyed saying very little and Lyn took pleasure in performing to another set of ears, their company was a frivolous relief. I needed the distraction as I was still very much torn between two worlds: adolescence and adulthood.

I left them and returned home. Entering the house, I used my small silver key attached to a chain with a bright green jewel, as green as onyx. Philly's taped-up boxes, having moved only six feet, sat guiltily on the stairs, knowing full well, when they did make a move it would be a huffy ascent to the loft.

Philly had now turned his attention to cooking, consequently he was arguing with a French recipe for *boeuf bourguignon*. He had only half the ingredients and at this weekend hour he would have to opt for alternatives. The clock on the mantel-piece chimed five o'clock. Bette would be leaving Claudie and returning home. I still could not fathom why we had not gone together, perhaps she felt I should be socialising with my peers and it was not always healthy to follow like a pilot fish to her every destination. She was wrong. If she'd asked, I would have followed her to the moon and back.

Part VII

In 1967, the 28th of October fell on a Saturday, three days before All Hallow's Eve. It was a fresh morning. The high, soft clouds were tinged a rosy pink and suspended in the air like a cluster of spaceships. In the five minutes it took me to wake and rise, the sun's position lay poised between rest and motion. As I began to dress, so the light began to strengthen and in equal measure we both evolved into the new day.

Bette had left her silent tread to start baking at *la boulangerie* next door. Philly was tapping on my door with the prospect of an enlightening experience. He was eager to make haste, knowing all too well how distracting the drifting scents of hot bread and pastry ignited hunger pangs and consumed concentration.

The previous evening, he had mentioned visiting the old walled cemetery of Collioure, close behind the market square, in a moderately quiet and peaceful spot, lined with tall pines. Together, we secured an early departure for two extremely valid reasons: one, *"a full contemplative atmosphere,"* and two, *"a service and ceremony were taking place at 11am,"* Philly had meaningfully put forth. There were no longer burials in the graveyard; the deceased were cremated and placed in their family's mausoleum.

We left the house without a word. Philly had picked a couple of rosemary sprigs from the pots in the courtyard. When we descended into town from the hillside route, and in clear view of the cemetery, Philly said, *"the rosemary's for remembrance... in my mind, it's always important to leave something. It says 'I came for you, I give to you.'"*

I saw a new side to Philly that morning, he had an awareness of grief and of loss and of how to respect and uphold these emotions. Not only did he speak grandly of science and of the universe, he felt strongly of the afterlife and of the soul. Anything you could not see or touch, he invoked his own ideas and theories. *"The body is gone... the spirit is left to find its place."* Philly determinately believed his philosophies were truths, although not pressing with his ideas and aesthetics, he was convincing. You could not help but fall for his passion of thought, rather than the thoughts themselves. He was not a religious man yet he understood the personal value and esteem of faith in a conviction not easily reasoned or rationalised. This freeness of spirit and liberty of mind was the reason for many lost lives and suppressed countries.

I followed him through the open gate, two paces in his shadow, as if he dragged some invisible sympathy on which I dare not step. Often, I thought how unique and special Philly and Bette were, sometimes seeing a bit of Bette in Philly and a bit of Philly in Bette. Understanding, in my maturing way, how they were similar enough to match and different enough to mesmerise.

I kept my head low. Philly led me to a small area with a central flagpole. The flag of France hung limp and lifeless, not a breath of air could lift it. Eight white wooden crosses in gravelled stone surrounds marked the graves: *carre militaire, tombes de soldats, morts pour la France.* On each cross read the name of a young man, his age and date of death. Here lay Collioure's sons, one as young as 18. The soldier's battles of World War I and II. Philly placed a rosemary sprig beside 'Massegu, Michel:' 9th August 1947, aged 24 years, exactly 20 years ago.

"I met his mother... the August just gone, she'd returned for his anniversary," Philly broke a hard silence, *"said she wouldn't come again, too old to make the trip. She had dark swollen eyes... cried every day for him, she'd said. Dear lady was rigid with pain. I won't forget her face though, she was the symbol of so many mothers... one War, two Wars."*

Philly sniffed, his soft sentimental statements echoed across the tombs. He turned abruptly, I followed in his wake, sailing the sorry wave of sadness. There could have been no better place for a reflection of history. His explanation of the sorrow and catastrophes to besiege this region would begin here.

Philly walked slowly, considering his words. *"During World War II this area was Vichy France, although it must be said there was a strong under-current of The Resistance. The Germans built gun emplacements along the seafront, widened and hardened the roads for their tanks... just outside our house they rolled along the coastline to Port Vendres suppressing both shoreline and spirit. The frontier lines, the guarded borders, the mountains and forests, all were heavily occupied."*

Philly continued. *"Then there was the influx of refugees at*

Argelès, escaping the endless persecution by Franco and his fascist Spain. Hundreds of thousands of desperate Spaniards flooding over the mountains into France. No haven for them though... stranded in makeshift camps, some even rounded up and sent off on the trains to face their fate in concentration camps. I'm sorry to say the French officials complied with orders from their German occupiers. Many of these refugees died, few survived... it's a miracle they were ever able to rebuild a life. The intense misery and degradation, trying to flee one war, only to be trapped by another. And still Franco rules over Spain."

Several swallows flew overhead, their pointed wings, their wild, free attitude. How incredible would it be to have a pair of wings, to escape to any clime and set up home safely. Suddenly my feet felt heavy, being only human I was tied down to Earth by weighty sandbags. However smart or bright my mind, if I was trapped, the ability to escape lay with my two feet alone. I was glad of them, but a pair of wings were the true attribute of freedom.

"It's a beautiful place here Mothy but it's seen such intense personal suffering... a land that has witnessed much pain."

My voice stuck on silent, my face still, my mind lost in an air of compassion and empathy for these poor souls. I wished for wings.

"Come," he smiled, *"let me show you someone else. Where there's melancholy, there's poetry!"*

A large, colourful, raised gravestone lay surrounded by Catalan and Spanish flags; small pots of flowers and rolled up papers, cards and a little post-box for messages, all highlighted the pilgrim's site. Three very tall and bushy silver-green trees shaded the space. I rubbed the fir between my fingers, it smelled of a sweet oil. Light knobbly cones were scattered on the ground below amongst older shreds of brown and sun-scorched pine.

Philly translated the inscription, the months were written in Roman numerals, *"Antonio Machado, born Seville, 26th July 1875, died Collioure, 22nd February 1939, and Ana Ruiz, mother of the poet, born Seville 4th February 1854, died Collioure, 25th February 1939."*

Philly continued his lesson with what he knew. *"Antonio Machado is, and was, the great poet of Spain. He was also an active republican, outspoken and artistic. Not a secure position to hold under Franco's repressive dictatorship... as you can imagine, so he had to flee his homeland. He laboured over the Pyrenees, travelled to exhaustion, physically and mentally worn down... as you can imagine. He was consumed by illness and dead two weeks later."* Philly paused, resting his eyes on Ana Ruiz. *"Three days later his mother joined him, it's said she died of a broken heart... as you can imagine."*

I noticed in the last breath Philly had said *"as you can imagine"* three times. Did it help to soften the blows of such great sadness and personal tragedy? Did he want to transport me back to this time almost 30 years ago.

"He lived in Casa Quintana, beside the river... it's always been shut up." Philly added and then he changed voice from unembellished to emotional.

"The wind, one brilliant day, called to my soul with an aroma of jasmine..." He stopped. *"Of course, he wrote the poem in Spanish but I've read a good English translation."*

Philly turned to exit. *"Have you ever smelt a jasmine bush, Mothy?"*

It was a rhetorical question.

"They're at their best in Spring, late March. The scent is so pungent and exotic, you sense them before you see them... a heady mix. Most of the jasmine in Collioure is a common variety, also known as poet's jasmine!" Philly drew a small laugh and I copied him. As we left the cemetery I glanced over my shoulder at poet Machado's grave. There, Philly had lain his second rosemary sprig.

On the short route home, we shared a hot, crusty baguette. We walked side by side, my head down, staring at my feet and Philly's brown shoes. It felt good to be grounded, to be able to walk away, making steps into a safer and more secure future, as safe as I understood it to be.

Part VIII

The temperate climate of South-West France is more clearly defined than that of Southern England. It offers a spring and autumn mix of high winds, rain and warm sunshine; scorching hot, dry summers; colder winters with occasional and always unexpected snowfalls. During my three months, from October rolling through into December, the temperatures dropped and the light weakened and we were restricted to the indoors or else faced the impending wrath of the elements, exposed, as we were, living on the coastline. Philly used to study the sky daily, particularly when it presented *'an interesting scape.'* He determined when the heavy, damp clouds would deliver rain and whether they would sit overhead by the force of an off-shore wind or develop at sea, which would later generate a stormy bay and 10-foot waves lashing at the harbour arm. It is not easy for any southern French man or woman to accept the inevitable steady decline into darker periods of weather, they live with an inbred entitlement to sun.

Philly called it, *'the weather retreat, with sporadic twists,'* for some brave locals were *'swimming in the bay up until early December, on account of a mild sea current.'* Then I remember he winked at Bette and added, *'the wonderful thing about the weather is, you never can tell precisely what it'll bring each season.'* Bette looked surprised and then disappointed, wiggling her earrings as Philly continued to lecture. *'During the winter the sun's rays struggle to burn through the clouds, they hit the Earth's axis at a shallow angle, the rays are more spread out and the heat energy more dispersed. Oh! but when the sun breaks through, it's worth running outside to grab the various spots in town where the warmth falls. With long nights and short days, we must take what we can.' 'There's one such cosy place in our front room, if we're lucky enough to catch it, where the sun lingers around mid-morning!'*

Philly said his piece and I listened enthusiastically. Bette was acting proud.

In late November Madame Simkin was seen walking Paul on the Nature Reserve, with its 360-degree layered view of the tumbling foothills of the Pyrenees and the blue-bleached Mediterranean expanse. The precipitous cliff face is a perilous drop to death and prone to sharp gusts and dizzying airs. Madame Simkin believed she was indestructible as well as indispensable and picked the most turbulent and unpredictable days to stray in high, rural country. Paul always returned a sodden heap and Madame's hair was as wild as the white horses at sea.

On a Sunday, after a blustery market, Philly and Bette, who had found the agitating winds disquieting, took me to Les Templiers. I had heard Les Templiers referred to by Claudie as the place Bette and Philly had met but I hadn't ventured in. I'd wandered past the entrance a few times but the interior was barrel-brown and the glass windows had simply reflected my own inquisitive face.

Les Templiers translates as The Knights Templars: a 12th century Christian military order of the wealthiest, most powerful and highly skilled fighters, many of whom passed through this region. They were closely linked to the Crusades, built Castles, defended the Christian faith and made pilgrimages to the sacred sites of the Holy Land.

Today Les Templiers is merely a name, and a reminder of the history of generations past. Later, through the years, I came to learn, in books, articles, and by a sort of osmotic gossip, the marvellous and fundamental facts of this focal point, central to the *'calling destination'* of Collioure. The present building is a hotel, café, bar and bistro and it is the immediate state and form of the place in which my great interest now lies. Within these walls a more recent story has been performed.

Stepping inside, Philly ordered Bette and me a hot drink and we sat at one of the wooden tables, deep inside. We gazed at the paintings hung haphazardly on the walls and narrow staircase. Each picture had been accepted by the owner, traded by tired and hungry artists who could not afford to pay for a drink or night's accommodation in one of the basic white-washed rooms.

What I speak of now I did not know aged 16. Knowledge and history have a certain way of finding you. The learning you undergo at school grows with you and at different stages gains a greater personal relevance, making life richer and at last full of tangible detail.

In 1905, making his way, from Collioure's provincial train station, to the heart of the small Catalan fishing village, walked Henri Matisse, a popular and active painter in his mid-thirties. He was searching for the inspiration lying in the light and the possibilities of colour. He was keen to express his creative visions, irrationally too, without the restrictions of formality. The works, Matisse and fellow companions produced, used dissonant colours and proclaimed untamed emotions. These inharmonious and incongruous new ideas - pink sea, red sand, yellow rooftops - were exciting. Matisse's self-indulgence collected some unnecessarily aggressive criticism, nonetheless he presented his beliefs and encouraged friends to take advantage of the effects of the effervescent light. He wrote to his young friend André Derain, *'venez'* – you must come. The colours of Collioure were *'sticks of dynamite'* and together they would use every pigment as never seen before. They would liberate colour, as if it had been trapped in time and allow it to burst onto the canvas in strong, simple shapes and forms. This kaleidoscopic vision, violent intensity of hues and flamboyant spontaneity would shock the complacent Paris Art World. Unrestrained and uncivilised, they painted as if the paints had never lived, they released the colours, alive with vitality and passion.

The chateau, the beached working boats, the shuttered interiors, the open bay, each image became wild and exuberant. If it wasn't bright yellow, or aubergine purple or patterned exotically, it was now. Nothing was meek or feeble, fine-lined or exact. The palette was thick, rich and glossy, the brushstrokes were quick and vigorous, achieving space, perspective, distance and light within light. The two men worked closely together, easel to easel, Derain was a great source of succour to Matisse, who was often plagued by depression and doubts and a wavering sense of self-belief.

Imagine Les Templiers in the early 1900s, the air thick with smoke from nicotine-heavy cigarettes and set alight with emotional outbursts, fierce debates and discussions on what to paint, where to stand or to sit, *'en plein air,'* which brushes to use, what textiles and fabrics to include, what wonderful vista to impress on next. The arguments must have been heated and stimulating, back and forth, curving through the air like imagination's rainbow. Maybe too, it was arrogant and intolerant, but it was happening, something sensational was being formed. This new era in art came from their fingertips and their brushes. Although short-lived and, with or without approval, these wild beasts of Fauvism would leave an indelible imprint on The Art World.

Drawn like a magnet, the lively and ebullient Willy Mucha painted his life in Collioure, entertaining and adding to the town's repertoire of the exotic. Mucha was *'crazy about the light.'*

To be *'crazy about the light'* was a phrase I recall Bette using early one evening as we sat on the beach. The sun slept on the horizon bed, the infinite sky glowed, a multitude of pinks burst and the landscape turned its famed vermillion red, before darkening and clearing the day of its sweep and substance. Bette had said. *"Many generations fall upon Collioure, most for the same reason: the light. We're just born into different times... oh for you it is to study French... but doesn't the whole atmosphere*

here lift you Mothy?"

It was true I did feel so much better by the sea, in the warm sun of late autumn, and I was certain I'd grown too.

In 1924, years after the Fauves had departed, Charles Rennie-Mackintosh, in his mid-sixties, in ill-health and accompanied by his red-haired wife Margaret entered Café Des Sports, as Les Templiers was then known. Margaret had kept a diary, describing Collioure as *'one of the most wonderful places we have ever seen.'*

A year earlier they had escaped the damp, smoggy industrial air of Mackintosh's studios in London to find inexpensive accommodation, just along the coast in Port-Vendres. Here *'the happiest and sunniest days of (his) life,'* were spent, forming an artistic relationship with the town and its environs. The warmth and the continual light were inspirational: *'dear Toshie is absorbed in his landscape,'* and his love for the colour *'green, green, green.'* By now Mackintosh had exchanged a career in architecture and design, to work with the fluidity of watercolours. His path of paintings in this area confirm this transition showing an affiliation between natural and man-made landscapes. Aware of his impatience and love of the land, he said of himself, *'I find my hands, when my mind is searching for some shape or form, squeezing green out of a tube - and so it begins again.'*

So here we were now in the winter of 1967, sheltering from a wind-swept day and sipping the last dregs of a powdery hot chocolate. Philly gestured to the bar, *"it's made of half a barque."*

Then up he jumped, inviting me to join him. *"Sleek and smooth, oiled with linseed,"* he said, running his hands along the side, *"a barque is a fishing boat."*

"Yes," I replied, to emphasise I was following his statements.

"In this case a retired and restored half," Philly strolled to the bow, *"with a beautiful and tenderly carved figurehead of a mermaid, holding a suckling child."*

Then he darted to the other end, close to the entrance and my head swivelled with him.

"Look Mothy!" Philly pointed and the bar-tender moved to his left. *"A signed photo of Picasso with René Pous, it's about where you're standing."* I shuffled over to his side. The image was faintly dated *1959* with a pen sketch of a reclining nude, the buttocks rounded, the body generous.

Philly resumed in a lower tone, *"The Pous famille are, and were then, owners of Les Templiers. René was the ever-hospitable, charming and welcoming host."* Philly scoured the wall behind the bar, then his eyes glowed, *"That's Pauline, his wife, she's a fine-looking woman, and well-painted. Together they socialised with entertainers, artists of the day... this place bursting with song, in the good years."*

The plainly framed painting of Pauline hung high on the top wall, longer and wider than the other portraits. Against a background of green, she wore, with an authoritative look, a bright yellow chemise. Her stern expression was accentuated by bushy eyebrows, thick hair and lips, pinched red. *Balbino Giner*, the artist had captured her skin with a smooth, pale well-lit fore-head. The impact was striking, but it was her eyes outlined in a heavy handed black, staring out directly at you, assessing and questioning, as they had done to everyone since the painting's completion in 1948.

"And Picasso?" I queried, returning to the photo and sketch.

"He came, like the others before him... to immortalise Collioure's harbour. There's something magnetic about this place... I believe it every day... appealing on so many levels." Philly turned to enjoy a view of Bette. She seemed distracted.

"She looks like she's on another planet," Philly said to my ear. He didn't mean anything he said to be unkind. Sometimes he did too much surmising and saying, he forgot to think. Bette remained still, her eyes read another story.

Philly and I returned to the table. Bette suddenly walked purposefully to the far-wall. Leaning in to study the works more closely, she endeavoured to hide and calm her obvious surprise. There was seldom an awkward time between the three of us, but for a short and seemingly significant moment, a silence hung. Philly and I waited. As time settled Philly turned his head to locate Bette; she remained deeply absorbed in the paintings.

"She's blinded by the light of a spectacle," said Philly

poetically with an undertone of knowing exactly what that feeling stirred. Like Bette, Philly was an enigma, leaving one unsure whether he understood the ambiguity of his words.

At this point in my tale I must include a letter I received from Bette, many years later, reflecting on this first afternoon inside Les Templiers. Her words and viewpoint give a perspective I could not explain; they are part of making her the extraordinarily particular person I longed to interpret.

Dear Mothy,

It's November again. The weather has turned bitterly cold. The snow fell heavy and thick on Mount Canigou, exceptionally early this year. In a positive mood, the run-off in Spring will be plentiful, but for now we must prepare for the rawness of winter.

The other day we were at Les Templiers, Simone joined us for a coffee and sends you her good wishes. Julian, is almost 8, he's quite a handful. Philly does his best to entertain him but Julian dotes on his mother. Philly ended up reading 'The Adventures of Tintin' books to himself. He's good at the voices and almost tempted Julian back into the fold of his arms.

There are one or two new acquisitions on the walls of Les Templiers including a cubist still-life of a mug and fruits, and a new scene of the market square in pastels. Did you tell me you made a drawing when you came here last? There is a three-quarter length portrait of Julian in a red jumper, rivetted by a book - apparently, it took hours to complete. He's a fidgety child but adorable too. The painting sits close by 'Madame Pous en jaune' whom they encased in glass and re-located lower down, near to the tables. Being by the artist Giner, it has, of late, attracted some attention. The last few summers have seen a surge in tourism. Philly is not pleased; he detests the littering and ill-disciplined behaviour of the holidaying students who are increasingly unruly in August, 'with too much time on their hands and too little to do.' He wants me to tell you these are his words!

The other day Philly was moving (not sorting!) boxes in the attic and he found my old collection of diaries tucked away. This discovery has spurred me on to write to you - I find writing very therapeutic. I prefer the permanency of the pen in matters of great importance, over the transitory passing of the spoken word, so often lost to surroundings.

In November 1967, when you were just 16, I'd made a long note of our visit to Les Templiers. Something happened that afternoon, you saw a change come over me. You made no comment, you were too polite and I was too vulnerable to tell. Remember I was still fairly young to Collioure's sites. I'd not even passed a full year of its seasons.

What caught my attention were two serene and subtle paintings, hanging side by side, opposite me, and going by the style, by the same unknown artist. My hand is shaking as I bring to mind what they evoked in me. Let me describe them: firstly, a medium-sized image of soft oils on canvas. There are two women on a large, tiled terrace, overlooking the town of Collioure. One wears a necklace of green stones and the other a straw hat with a bow. Why they could be

*Simone and me! Beyond their balcony rises the clocher, in
some paintings it is called le phare, and the sweep of bay
with white sails departing the harbour, a sight synonymous
with our perception of this place. The curl of the landscape,
the protruding hillside, the distant olive groves and the
distorted vines are all the features we recognise today,
even though we have a new construction now ashamedly
dominating. It is the two women, quite identical, as the
title suggests, in dress of the late 1940s on which I focus
Mothy, because I know them! Or rather I knew them. They
really existed - their faces, their mannerisms, they are from
my past. They made the trip here as I chose to do. I must
have been about 11 when they left and took voyage in June
1948. The full moon fell that year on the 21st and in my
spell here, I have never seen them. One day I'll explain what
all this means.*

*Beside this painting, labelled 'Les Dames Jumelles,'
(The Twin Ladies) hangs the second, a small companion
piece. The unsigned artist has, with difficulty but distinct
awareness, painted a full moon rising in a deep, azure-blue
sky with milky clouds and, significantly, a bolt of light
that flashes across the heavens. I am transfixed by it. It is
entitled Solstice d'Ete 1948 (Summer Solstice). The artist
has captured the rare phenomenon of a full moon on the eve
of the Summer Solstice and the dazzle and illumination
spread aloft is Ather's pod entering. I have to put this in*

writing now and allow you to wait for me to write the whole story. Perhaps you'll one day start a memoir with my final letter! Whoever knows?!

All I told Philly, in honesty of the occasion in November 1967 was my specific interest in these two beautiful paintings. Well, for my birthday this year he bought me the two pieces, framed. It is normally the custom at Les Templiers not to sell any of the pictures. Philly had made a special request and they agreed.

'All of life comes to Collioure, and we always find it in Les Templiers,' Philly made a poignant observation. He said to me quite earnestly, 'the paintings should belong to you, their artistry made you glow and from this you gain strength.' The same day we hung them above the mantel-piece in the front room.

With my love Mothy, Bette x

In the course of our late Sunday morning at Les Templiers, many other local characters passed in and out through its doors. There were travelling artists with their cart, easel and paints; couples with young, squabbling children; *dames et messieurs* breaking their daily promenade; the occasional table for one, reading the paper or writing a note. By now I was familiar with some *Colliourencs* (a localised term used to describe an inhabitant of Collioure and part of the vernacular). I didn't know them by name, only by the regular faces I had become accustomed to seeing; the meeting with a mutual nod of head as a sign of friendly acknowledgment and acceptance. Eventually residents and associates of the town, who have no name to you, merely a face and appearance, become remarkably easy to spot in new scenarios. Marcel, the chef at Chez Simone and Jacques, Simone's waiter, came to collect boxes of wine for the restaurant. Jacques recognised Bette instantly, although she was oblivious to his stare, and seeing that Philly and I had identified him, he smiled courteously. The barman then handed him a heavy case of wine marked *'vin blanc - fragile.'* Jacques had a young haughtiness and arrogance; he needed to be careful or he'd find himself in trouble. With Philly, I felt, by the force or eye-contact, we'd trimmed the youth's swagger, at least for this day. On reflection, his pride was sometimes overbearing, but it was the enormous self-confidence Jacques displayed that provoked a little envy in me.

Philly had once said, in generalisation, although I knew he based his idea on Jacques, *'sometimes there's a twist of irony lying beneath confidence in that the person deep-down lacks the self-belief they exude... pluck and aplomb make up for not having it at all.'*

'So, sort of like acting... by giving yourself a quality or feature you don't have, pretending or lying?' I said.

'Well yes and no, lying is too extreme. Self-preservation might be better said. Perhaps we all, publicly, hide away a bit of our true selves... would that be a misrepresentation or falsity to do so? Oh, and remember we are all viewed differently by different people.' Philly tapped his head. I had thought the same myself after my own time with Claudie.

Philly was wise with words and thought, often trailing off and presenting questions he still could not take firmly to a conclusion. I do not think he was intent upon a resolution. He understood the world was a mystery and so were people, not one alike, each one a secret, both on the outside and to themselves.

While Philly went to check on Bette's well-being, I went outside, having recognised Louis and Michael dawdling on the steps, trifling away their time as they did most weekends with little to distract them.

The winds had dropped a notch and the sky sucked of grey cloud and bother. With the afternoon brightening before the prevailing loss of light, doors were opened and so it seemed everyone from my French class had come calling at Les Templiers. Opposite the main entrance was a setting of outdoor tables and chairs under a strongly fitted awning. The area, housing roughly 12 tables, possessed the same blue colourings and typeface, marking it the reserve of Les Templiers customers. Louis, Michael and I sat together and began a trend of hopeful youths. Hannah concealed having spotted us from the corner of her eye and sat diagonally opposite with two older French boys. I guessed she felt safer knowing we were there but, as was her custom, she refused to acknowledge us. I was incapable of reading her hair-actions: flicking it left to right, right to left, bunching it behind her head or plaiting it at the side. She was smoking a cigarette in a fashion that read it was a social necessity in order to mark her above us children. I made observations and played with objective opinions. I left her coded habits, for Hannah was a live-wire, as unpredictable as a firework.

Into view also came Lyn, talking at the top of her voice, and Gen, shaking her head and sculpting a deep frown of disagreement. They were arguing. Gallantly charging up behind was the appeaser, Edward, rolling his eyes and trying to cool the storminess. In a painting, he'd have been the sunshine trying to part the clouds, or the wind eager to blow the two foes from their howling clash. This time they were vehemently opposed over something, though both were sensible enough not to bring reinforcements into their altercation. They rushed past. When Jenny, who was skipping behind Edward, slipped and fell on the misshapen stones with a bruising thud, everyone, excluding Hannah, ran to her rescue. The feuding dispute dissolved into the air. We took Jenny down to the sea, she was sobbing and shaky. I was sorry for her pains, yet secretly pleased I could pull out of my pocket a large, white handkerchief to soften her shock. She bathed her knees in the saltwater, we all did, to share in the discomfort. It was numbing, cold and sharp underfoot.

On shore, I handed her a stone, saying *"put your tears, and your aches and pains into this stone and throw them out to sea."* And so she did.

"Feel better now?" I asked. She nodded and raised the corner of her mouth to one side, a half-smile.

Lyn came darting over. *"Of course she does, sea works magic. We took Pat, my brother, down to sea when he cut his finger, healed quick as ever, forgot he'd even hurt it!"* She babbled.

For once, I wished she wasn't in every frame, her kindness a combination of care and competitiveness. She was convincingly worldlier and more seasoned than any of us; it was sensible not to compete, better to find your own particular niche.

"Come on Jenny, Gen and I will help you back."

The clocher struck a single dong, a half hour after the o'clock. It was 3.30. We all parted and headed our separate ways. The sun was lowering, another two hours of light expected. Philly and Bette were leaving Les Templiers; I took a market bag from under Bette's arm. Silently we strolled home, each consumed by distinct and separate reveries: those untouched stories of the mind.

Part IX

The topic arose when we took a picnic to the rugged area, high above town. Out in the open air the mind is freer. There are no walls to contain what is said and you can sit with a sense or a memory for as long as you choose. The distractions are fewer, the elements build a bigger world: swaying boats, floating birds, the busyness of people. Yet what's been said and shared is still real, still registered. Without the fresh surrounds and comforts of nature, in which to react and interact, less would be revealed of our own nature. At the picnic, the topic arose.

It was a weekday and, apart from my own aforementioned sick day, the only other day I found myself at odds with the week was the Friday Madame Simkin fell ill. I was fit at least and with an extra day added onto Sunday, suddenly at leisure. Madame Simkin was suffering an irritable cough, it had begun late Thursday. By Friday morning a tight, dry, scratchy voice was straining to conjugate a series of irregular verbs. Her pockets were stuffed with hankies, dipped in neat eucalyptus oil; the exotic whiff made even Paul keep his sniffy distance. Small staccato coughs and a swollen, tickling red nose had enveloped her. She was fighting an awful infection making it hard to comprehend her; she gargled words like you might a throat tincture. We feared for our own welfare, early winter colds were difficult to elude and would take weeks to shake off. It was Hannah who offered, with a fine theatricality unknown to

Madame, to visit the pharmacist on her behalf. The favour was politely declined. Although we all knew any favour delivered from the lips of Hannah was calculated to be advantageous to herself. Madame Simkin was not accustomed to the self-serving ways of a teenager, perhaps the generation gap helped seal her oblivion. A group of young workmen were renovating the upper floor of a three-storey hotel close to *la pharmacie*. Hannah was always willing to exert her expertise in the powerful effects of femininity over the male. Unless someone could tame her, difficulties could arise and who'd be there to help her when she'd dismissed everyone so callously.

The afternoon lecture which read on the noticeboard as *'Vignerons et Vignobles de Monsieur Eugene Bernard'* was cancelled despite the fact Madame Simkin played no role in the oration. Quite frankly she was our overseer and if she could not instruct the afternoon's address, then the afternoon could not proceed. On leaving class I held the door open as Madame sneezed through the exit, *"Merci Mothy Paul,"* she gestured. Paul, her dog, reluctantly shuffled his body in time to catch the swing of the door, and out they tottered together.

Our Friday afternoon eased into Saturday, then lapsed into Sunday. The unhurried, casual hours flowed to the natural rhythm of a weekend's repose. Then came Monday, the start of the week, without structure, without routine, without obligation. It was either Philly or Bette, on this occasion I forget which, who made the most of the situation and re-designed Monday for the three of us.

It was the penultimate Monday before the closing of November. I had, roughly, another four weeks in Collioure, the week before Christmas, and then the coming of a New Year. Keeping a check on dates rolls me through the calendar around which all stages of our life are cycled and controlled.

Philly's final project of the year involved the Christmas Fair in the Chateau. For this, he agreed, he had ample time. It was currently scheduled to begin the 20th December, two days after I returned to England. Bette's boulangerie shift was operating its late winter hours by closing all Monday and half a day Wednesday with reduced stock. Bette said Pavia (*la famille de boulangers*) kept her on out of kindness and loyalty, especially after the death of a family member in June. The circumstances of which were unbearable, so very respectively, grief and sorrow were shared, help was received and friendship, kinship and solidarity were shown. *'It was in the doing, not the saying,'* Bette had said of those early days.

Our picnic location lay up a steep hill, northwards out of town. It overlooked the commandoes' headquarters, an old prison building. The school of the French Army had been stationed in Collioure since 1964. On this day ten open-backed army vehicles waited to transport the men away for a day of mountain manoeuvres.

Behind our position grew low, puffy bushes, the wind slipped through their stems like hair through a comb. There were wandering seeds, pretty flowers of weed-like quality and many olive saplings. Parts of the land were free to campers; July and August were the active months. By the time the last weekend of August arrived, the campsites were bare, the travellers were packed and gone and the parched patches of grass and tatty bushes were free to gather strength and grow again. Philly had chattered as we walked the sharp incline to the secluded spot. Below us lay a fine view of the town, curving down to the sea and wrapping around a perfect silver-licked shoreline, sparkling like ice crystals on an ice-lolly.

It was an odd day for Bette, which makes me think it was perhaps Philly who'd organised the picnic jaunt. I did not watch her purposely. Living as close as we were you cannot help sense a vibe or pick up an emotion, as well as the mannerisms that catch each of us. She was a beautiful woman with a busy, sunny manner and a deep kindness I was happy to share. However, I doubt on this day, not even she could have analysed herself, who she was or what she felt. She was completely out of sorts, everything a contradiction or a quandary. Every daily matter made her tearful: the dew-wet grass, a dry plant pot, a chipped nail, a cracked wall tile, a diving cormorant at sea, a red cheek, a pale cheek, a napkin in the wrong drawer, a limp flower in a vase, dust where she dusted, socks washed twice and caught up the sleeve of a shirt, the sun too bright, the sun behind a cloud. Everything adjusted correctly, everything out of line. On the kitchen table, she lifted up a dirty coffee cup, wiped the surface clean underneath and placed it back down again. What a mixture, she must have had twenty thoughts for every male's one. Her mind exhausted me: mixed up, disjointed, confused. I gave her concerned glances. Philly was diverted by the potential weather conditions. Nonetheless she approached the picnic quietly and attentively, having packed a choice of cheeses, cured hams, a *'baker's dozen'* of baby potatoes and leftover bread she learnt to keep fresh by wrapping in wax paper and then a paper bag.

Finding a sheltered spot, we settled comfortably on our picnic hillside. Despite the tranquillity of the view and gentle warmth I sensed Philly had lost his appetite for constant conversation. He'd puffed and exhausted enough air, so dug for a question to last the majority of time outdoors. Sensing I was the entertainer, Philly struck well. *"How did you come to choose the language, French?"* As he asked me, a thin slice of meat dangled from his mouth like a second tongue, he did look funny. He caused a small smile to lighten Bette's face. It didn't solve the mystery inside her, but certainly relaxed the previous awkwardness.

My response was unintentionally long, yet with hindsight, it proved an interesting one for my two listeners: foreigners to the lands and life I knew so well. I also realised once again, those days I had left in England were gone. On my return, life and work would be facing a new direction, I'd be moving at a new pace. My experience in France was ready to alter me.

Philly turned his ears to listen and Bette edged inwards. I recall now, as my adult self, the story I gave them.

"It was nearing the end of this year's summer term. My closest friends, by nickname, Olly, Lymy, and Woof, and I were finishing our exams. We each had about nine or ten

subjects, I did nine. The modern language exams, I took only French, are split into four parts: reading, writing, listening and oral. The oral part is always set later than the other sections, no-one knows why, it means we have to wait ages to finally complete 25% of the exam. We were told, 'this was the way of The Board.' By the time the 22nd of June came, all our examinations were over and so it was Woof who suggested we all met at the top of Battle Hill. It was that same day we would say well done, farewell and celebrate the end of this significant school year.

Battle Hill is a large mound, located beyond the oak woodland and playing fields but still within the school premises. It's the only permitted location where you cannot be seen by any teacher. We'd been there on and off at weekends, but rarely as a group of four. There were rumours, spread in the first-year's term, surrounding the mound and even if you didn't believe the tales, there was something peculiar about the place. It was said the mound was filled with the bodies of soldiers who'd met their fate at too young an age. Secretly the dormant bodies were still brimming with life and energy. It explained why the grass was always a vivid green, even in winter, and never grew wild or disorderly. The spring tulips flowered early and lasted over three months. Every year they appeared in different places, their petals painted with a variety of patterns and mixed colours as if they annually reinvented their costume. The birds recognised the uniqueness of this place and, displaying their innate respect, flew to either side of the Hill, never over the top.

So, it was agreed. Olly was keen, I remember that. We had no responsibilities, and soon we'd be packed and gone.

We met in the dorm hallway at 7pm after supper and walked

94

out towards Battle Hill. We rarely felt a summer's heat, being so close to damp woodlands and shaded ponds. It was a clear, bright June evening. Woof noted, no rain had fallen since the 8th of June. I packed a jacket and rug. We were reminded throughout the day by exam-anxious teachers, it was the longest day of the year: The Summer Solstice. It spread like a light rash through school and helped keep our minds off the immediate task at hand: finally completing the examinations for which we had spent the last two years preparing. The oral date had sat penned on the calendar since the beginning of the second term in January. The thought of June and the end of exams had seemed an eternity away.

I did not see until the day after our escapade to Battle Hill, the large calendar pinned on the notice-board of the student hall, obediently open at June. It had a small white circle in the bottom right corner of the 22nd symbolising a full moon. Woof stood beside me and we looked at the symbols.

'Only once in a blue moon do the Summer Solstice and a full moon come together!' My maths teacher spoke boyishly, over my shoulder as I packed my belongings. He chuckled at his own clever use of words, probably releasing some of his nervous energy into factual humour.

'Of course the expression, 'once in a blue moon,' is a misnomer because a blue moon is when two full moons appear in the same month: one at the beginning and one at the end, so it turns out it's not that unusual.' He trailed off, making even the most interesting of statements seem dull.

I remember rain broke on the 23rd and over twice as much on the 25th. We were lucky with our night outdoors and what it would mean to us.

We didn't want to believe it would be the last night together before making our separate ways. In truth, all change was about to happen. The summer holidays would pass and already our lives were mapped differently.

We settled on Battle Hill in a world of our own and without a care in the world. Lymy brought a bag of toffee buttons and some Aztec bars: a combination of milk chocolate, nougatine and caramel. The toffee buttons had melted a bit, stuck together and when they hit the tongue, separated into chewy, sticky bits. Talking coherently was impossible, my teeth felt glued together and my jaw ached from laughing at the bizarre set of gobbledygook we spoke (I re-phrased this for Bette and Philly as incomprehensible sentences). We had to repeat everything until the syrup loosened and relieved the mouth!

Olly had hidden a transistor. We had a good wave-length on the hill, and were able to hear the records that would define the summer: Procul Harum's song 'Whiter Shade Of Pale' played on and on and The Beatles 'St Pepper's Lonely Hearts Club Band' was released. Through music we experienced a revolution. On the night of 22nd June our sensible, constricted selves were freely released. Lymy smoked his dad's Pall Mall cigarettes. They'd been sent from London with the note – 'better I know you have the best in hand!' The weather stayed warm, the light persisted. Pink, flying-saucer clouds spread skilfully and evenly like wallpaper across the open sky and then the full moon, large and bright materialised like a magic lantern. I spotted it first. Instinctively and without gesture we knew the night was unlike any other we would find again, for us this would be a pivotal moment in our lives. We decided we would each reveal our life-plan and ambitions to one another. All of life lay ahead and as the world expanded before us so our fields of interest narrowed.

Olly said he would be an apprentice to his father's workshop in ironmongery and welding, although he suspected he would have to learn a milder craft first such as pottery, his mother was a keen ceramicist. Lymy was interested in painting, particularly portraits and was always copying images by the great masters from books in the library or attempting to sketch teachers in class or any willing student. He even drew animals when the sheep with their lambs came out in spring to graze in the adjoining meadows.

Woof confessed he longed to fly. He had a collection of model aeroplanes and had spent previous holidays at Ferryfield, Lydd in East Sussex, watching passenger and freight operations and sneaking into private and general aviation lessons. There was no family relation in the Air Force. After our evening, seeing the sky so wide and luminous, he wanted to be free, high above birds and clouds, where he might find 'answers among the unexplainable.' Woof was already quite a cerebral and unconventional boy. If he was so out-of-the-ordinary then the sky seemed the best place for him. He believed it too.

I was the most undecided of our group. Learning French came with the opportunity to travel to France for 3 months, to absorb another culture and lifestyle, something I really wanted to do. My father was untouchable. My mother was merry and always with friends, having, in private, tried to recognise and rescue, unsuccessfully, my father's financial issues. Now she moved over to a new reservoir of untapped hobbies and found relief in free expression. There was kayaking in Scotland and yoga in the Lake District. Throughout the summer, cardboard boxes sat on the stairs at home waiting to be collected by someone for something: knitted baby jumpers to East Africa, cakes to the church hall for fund-raising, old clothes and toys to India (I secretly rescued a favourite old teddy before he made the trip abroad), pamphlets on lectures, brochures for excursions to the continent, tickets to the theatre in London, half day-tours to the coast, all inclusive. What I saw was a new lease of life, as my father slipped further into the dark. My brother Nico was popular, determined, if a little arrogant and headstrong. He filled any family gaps and delivered the social graces and was certainly capable of articulating for two. He was ready to start defining his career. I could slide away, probably unnoticed for a while at least, and return wiser and turn heads with my worldliness."

When I finally finished my piece, Bette had a numb arm from leaning in so closely and the intermittent gasps and huffs from Philly left me in no doubt as to his keen interest.

"You'll return a good man Mothy, what models we are, hey Bette!" Bette raised her head and smiled.

"You said, The Summer Solstice. It was a spectacular sight here too, all pinks and oranges, and silky blues. What a moon! You could polish your glasses and read the paper by its light, so dense in the sky it sat. We all remember where we were that night." Philly turned his head to Bette, encouraging a word from her. You could see him wondering why she was so reticent. What were her thoughts? If she uttered words and mindfulness into phrases, they could never be retrieved, so it pleased her to risk nothing at all, even amongst our safe circle of three.

"Bette arrived in Collioure on the 22nd. It was one of our first talking points at Les Templiers. I tried to impress her but simply ended up blathering about this and that." Then Philly tuned his voice to a high thespian tone, *"Oh how*

she struck me! A bolt out of the blue... so fine, so fine!"

Bette was embarrassed, she'd turned cold and wanted to go.

"Your story was very interesting Mothy," she whispered. *"I'm glad you came."* Her necklace shimmered.

"I'm glad you came too," I said. I thought to wink like Jacques had done, but the moment between us was worth more. She gave me one of her enchanting smiles, the happy energy warmed my face.

Philly, waiting some steps ahead, caught Bette looking backwards to where the flattened grass told of our picnic.

"Have you forgotten something?" He called mildly.

"No," She wavered, *"I shall not forget anything!"*

The same evening I played with her line in my head, *"I shall not forget anything, I shall not forget anything."* I fell asleep and my dreams spoke of Bette. I saw her as the Mona Lisa, the lady within the bluey-green *sfumato* landscape, alone in Le Louvre: enigmatic, curious, mystifying and something of a rarity.

Part X

It is just over 36 years since Woof disappeared over *'The Sleeve'* at its narrowest point: The Straits of Dover. *'The Sleeve'* is the English translation of the French, *La Manche*. This busy body of water separates Southern England from Northern France. During the War this was Britain's first and last line of defence and strategically most important barrier.

The Sleeve was the title Woof used when referring to The Channel. He often spoke in a vernacular either of his own creation, or he interpreted foreign words and included them in English conversation, sometimes leaving us guessing at a word's common or original meaning. We later described it as *'Woof's old-boy parlance'*. He had an interest in finding alternative words or substituting more frequently spoken ones with a version of his own liking. It was a particularly effective technique at school, when it was called *'school-boy tongue.'* It is he who devised our nicknames. Woof used his skill extremely well, writing small note-pad dictionaries of new words and phrases. It was a dialect he conceived, not dissimilar to home-talk when families share a familiar language or craft-jargon when certain terminology is used among work colleagues. As an example, Battle-hill was known to us as *'Bill's mound'* and if rain was forecast he'd cry *'cats and dogs 'til lunch,'* a double maths lesson to him was *'squared hell'*. Naturally he conversed in normal English. It was the occasional odd line or word that formed this code between us. Deciphering his secret language system helped pass the school hours and livened up the monotony of a Monday to Friday timetable.

Woof was vigilant and superstitious and would occasionally lie awake tapping his pencil, predicting the procedure of the following day's lessons or the weather or the forthcoming holiday, rarely living in the moment but preparing for the next; existing in secret worlds, his brain always alert and forward-thinking. I was almost certain he would be a journalist or writer of some merit. It was a surprise to us all when he announced he would enter the RAF. Yet again, this was precisely the way of Woof, just when you felt you knew his disposition and tendencies, he surprised you by choosing a whole other direction.

Lymy, Woof and I stayed on at Battles-gate until 18. Olly left in 1967, to join his father and then later bound through indenture to a master craftsman far North of the country. Only a few years later, when we were more firmly settled in our fields of work, did we re-establish regular contact. Lymy, Olly and I kept different occupations but the overlapping of our jobs allowed us to maintain a closeness. I moved around as warden for my Trust, much like Woof in the air-service, from Lincolnshire to Oxfordshire to Buckinghamshire.

There was not a county I didn't know well enough to find a cold pint and a local meal, within a 10-mile radius of my lodgings. To keep in touch, Woof and I found phoning each other a pointless task as we were both either out of range or moving from location to location. We did, however, uphold our friendship by sending postcards to the most suitable homing-address of the time and subsequently met three times a year at a pub convenient to us both. I continued to play the games Woof placed on our friendship. One year he chose coloured pubs: The Red Lion, The White Hart, The Green Man, then titles: The King's Head, The Queen's Crown, The Duke of Wellington.

In February 1980, we met at The Moon Pub in West Sussex. I had already turned 29 and Woof was 28. Woof had set the date, 29th of February; it was a leap year. Leap years held no special meaning to me, it was still a working day, the 29th marked a Friday. Herein I took note of future leap years.

The weather was heavy and the temperatures mild. There was nothing special about February's extra day, it made the dismal month 24 hours longer. Rain swept in from the Atlantic. A gusty blast of cold air disturbed the sitting room chimney, provoking a reaction by persistently whistling; it then badgered my efforts to complete tasks outside. The sluggish days of established winter zapped the spirit. Steam and warmth came only from hot tea and pub fires and even these stimulants fell short of their usual vigour. I felt all of my 29 years plus the inheritance of my father's despondency. This deficiency had set in over winter, it was slow to thaw and I was facing a lonely period of semi-hibernation.

However, the day's objective was to see Woof at 'The Moon Pub.' He was smartly dressed, sitting in a quiet crescent-shaped corner seat with high, red velvet cushioning, his pint half drunk. I ordered two more local ciders and we set about talking.

You may ask, what does this tangent of time in 1980 have to do with my tale of Bette and Philly? It is only now in my later years I see how some elements of my life form a connection. It is important I now join these significant events together to create a combined story.

Woof pulled out of his pocket a large, round, silver-faced watch with a black, rather worn, neatly stitched leather strap. *"My grandfather's watch,"* he said, *"he died about 7 years ago... someplace in France I can't pronounce. I'd never seen it before... it just turned up last Christmas."* He pinned it on his slender wrist and turned it side to side, *"just started wearing it. It's no ordinary device let me tell you, it has a complication."* He paused to add, with a touch of irony on his tongue, *"lunacy, you know!"* I remember he chuckled. It is true to this day, the unusual acquaintances I have made through life will, at some uncertain point, speak with ambiguity. Mostly I am slow to process it, but I always pick out lasting lines or phrases and keep them stored at the back of my mind until they spin forward into relevance. Woof meant lunacy in its true sense, 'madness' but also 'lunar' in relation to the moon.

Woof began to explain in detail the intricacies of his moon-phase watch; this was the fascinating timepiece he had inherited. I looked with interest at its unusual features and proportions and turned questioningly to him. He pointed at the dial and continued.

"A moon-phase watch displays the current phase of the moon as perceived in the sky. In general, the moon has four phases...

the phases are the lighted areas of the moon we see from Earth."

Woof enjoyed playing with the names, *"waxing gibbous, waning crescent."*

"My grandfather the eccentric! It may seem a curious device but observing the moon from new to full was the first and earliest method of showing the passing of a month." He continued, with the confidence of research, *"the sun deals with seasons, whilst the modern calendar, and not forgetting the ebb and flow of tides, are linked to the phases of the moon. Clever uh?!"*

I inclined my head to the clock-face, two silver dials, the gold face symbolising the glowing rock. Here we were pleasantly seated, yet really, scientifically, spinning through space orbited by the moon, dressing and undressing itself in the sky. In the 16th century periodic bouts of insanity were thought to be triggered by the moon. It was an interesting function. I opened my mouth, but nothing could be found to fill the silent void between the watch and the lesson.

A bar-maid slapped down some peanuts on the table, and I jumped.

"Them's just nuts!" She grinned. Woof picked up four peanuts, one he left whole, the others he re-designed, biting into them in a sufficient enough way to represent the moon phases.

Behind our booth at the window, a mist came visiting, bringing with it a silent rain, depositing itself mournfully on the peeling-white sill. Visibility was poor. The light was weak and had abandoned the ambition to rise. The forthcoming new month of March and its spring equinox was the only inviting proposal this 29th day of February could promise.

The heart of the pub was crowded. We appeared to exist in an untouched corner, as if a quarantine line marked us out as unapproachable. No matter. Our small room seemed to speak not in colours or style or configuration but in moods: pensive, lonesome, secretive. Woof was a distinctive man and completely unaware of his magnetism; he drew attention although strangely no one drew near to know him. He made an impression, though not one person could tell you who he was, or what he did. His attire described a lazy, country-lad of affluence, only I knew him to be an RAF pilot. If he'd been in uniform people would have known his role immediately but even this was a costume of sorts.

Woof's moon-phase watch struck a chord with me. I had seen one before, not in the flesh, but in a photo. This occurrence of such a fanciful item takes me once again back to Collioure in 1967 and back to Bette. I remember the day so clearly, although I made no word of it to Woof. There is nothing worse in life's exchanges when a good friend spoils your joys by admitting they've seen or done something before you.

It was a December week. A flurry of snow had turned

the peak of Mount Canigou a brilliant white. The mountain was sharp, crisp and as clear as crystal. If it had not been so popular with artists, who arrive to the fierce clarity of winter ready to capture Canigou's breath-taking scale, I'd have believed it a mirage. Were we all being fooled by an imaginary vision? In town, we relished the short days of sun. Philly used his spare time to sit in his calculated sunny patches.

It was the first Thursday of the month, the 6th. Madame Simkin arrived in a fraught state. The early winds of winter tugged at the air around her body and seemed to pick and push at her, she moved shaking this way and that as if she wished to throw it off. She was 20 minutes late, instead of her customary 40 minutes early, Paul yapping at her side, chasing her *foulard* as it slithered along the floor.

Her make-up was a peculiar sight, we all held a stifled giggle. The eye-shadow was lipstick-red and the lips wore an eye-shadow plum, some of Paul's poodle-fur was lodged in her hair.

We proceeded with lessons, structure and normality resumed.

At mid-morning break she sent me out for *'du lait à l'epicerie.'* In what was close to two and a half months of class, not one of us had run an errand for Madame. I was surprised at her request and that it should be me chosen to fulfil it. Nonetheless I quickly answered, *'mais oui Madame!'* Paul wanted to follow. He was stopped at the door by a heeled shoe, and returned to his bed to chew on a bit of scarf.

The outside bitterness was a fresh jolt to the senses; it ran down inside me, trickling like water through a pipe, until I could no longer feel where it ended. It was affective: raw, invigorating and dizzying. The streets were fairly empty. As I passed Les Templiers I peered into the dark interior, my hands to my forehead shielding the light outside from reflecting the surroundings. I squinted, and then moved closer, pressing up to the glass. I focused. Why, there was Bette, standing at the bar, leaning her slim frame over the polished wood, staring keenly at the photo of Picasso and René Pous, the one Philly had pointed out. It felt wrong to see her and not say anything. I was not spying yet without making my presence known I sensed the cold chill of a spy, an intruder in observation. The door made a dead slam as I entered. The few people seated at tables, sipping coffees, reading papers, smoking long cigarettes and gossiping like sparrows, looked up. Bette stared, fixated by the image on the wall. I coughed, still she didn't move. So I tapped her elbow everso gently, she turned, looking radiant and mesmerising. I'd seen her only a few hours earlier. Had I forgotten how beautiful she was in such a short time or did a new bloom emanate from her as if to cover her in another glory? Whereas most people communicate, naturally, with mouth and sound, Bette, spoke meaningfully through her eye-contact. This is harder to read as one must make guesses at context and purpose.

"I've had a surprise, Mothy." She spoke with bright, watery eyes.

Her eyes led me to the photo, then, with soft sound and firm intent she said, *"look at the photo Mothy..."*

"*Yes, I remember it, Picasso and Pous, they're looking right at us, they're standing somewhere in here... and the paintings on the walls and the sketch below and...*"

"*Look at Picasso... not his face... look at his arm.*" She said animatedly, but still quietly.

"*I'm looking... he's smoking something, he's wearing a watch?*" I replied, guessing.

"*Yes, yes, he's wearing a watch!*"

"*But that's nothing unusual.*"

Bette looked at me a little disappointed.

"*It's a special kind of watch... it's a moon-phase watch...*" She seemed so excited just saying the word, "*on the clock-face is a small function that displays the phases of the moon... as we see them in the sky... so if it's a full moon then the moon image is whole,*"

Bette spoke a little louder. "*Remember, on Friday last, the first, a new moon rose? We saw it together. While René Pous keeps his hands behind his back... look at the confidence of Picasso... cigar in hand, a sun-bronzed arm and the watch, right in the centre of the picture.*"

I wanted to be as enthused as her, but I couldn't find words. It seemed better not to say anything, to pause the atmosphere rather than to reply with something inadequate. I tried to lift my mood and expression to encourage her. She gazed upon the photo, absorbing the figures, imprinting the sight as if in future she might recall its conception as acutely to mind. We had passed less than ten minutes at the bar. Looking at my own dull, simple watch, the numbers 1-12 in black on a plain white background I realised instantly I had to return and take with me some milk for Madame.

"See you later Bette, I must fly... Madame is waiting."

"Yes, hurry back to class... oh, don't fly away!" She smiled. *"The wind has picked up... we must be spinning faster!"*

Bette did not raise the subject of the moon-phase watch again. The next time it was to land in my lap was when Woof began his story.

In December 1967, a new moon fell on the first day. Bette and I had watched it form a shiny smile in the sky, we imitated it childishly with our mouths. On New Year's Eve, a new moon rose once more, I sat at home in England, on a bench in the garden, wrapped in a thick rug. I thought of Bette and Philly, picturing where they might be. I chose two places: on the beach throwing stones, the light catching the ripples, or sitting by the edge of the chateau wall, keeping still with their bodies and busy with their thoughts.

In early May of 1980 a card arrived from Woof, he was evidently continuing his celestial theme, recommending our next *rendez-vous* be 'The Sun in Splendour' in London on the first of June.

Two days before we were due to meet I received a message forwarded to me at the lodge: *Jeffrey Barker, missing, presumed dead, over The Channel on an unscheduled night manoeuvre, date 29th May 1980.'* Its militaristic structure was as impersonal as it was brief. Shattering my almost childlike sense of expectation for our meeting, the tight wording contrasted horribly with the years of friendly openness Woof and I had shared.

The night Woof disappeared was a full moon and a well-lit sky. I could not speculate on what had happened, I was full of grief and anger.

It is now 2016 and I am 65 years old, nine leap years, including this year, have passed since our last meeting at 'The Moon Pub.'

Woof's parting words to me, *"See you in the sky!"* What did he mean? Was he referring to the next pub, or something far greater? My complex spiritual friend.

The problem with things far greater than our human understanding is they knock the senses of common-sensed people.

Part XI – I

It is about now in my story, you'll begin to wonder if I, Mothy Chambers, ever returned to Collioure. *'Did you return to Collioure Mothy, after your first affair with that magical, enchanting place? The place you could not stop talking about after you came home, in the security and comfort of friends, Lymy, Olly and Woof. Then inwardly and tentatively, tilting the head and speculating: what would Philly do, what would Bette think?'* Claudie would tell another one of her stories and I'd never know how it began or how it ended and she'd age and fade and forget me, until I was another spot on her horizon of memories, on whom she might pin a tale. Simone's café, Les Templiers bar, the cemetery, the chateau, the seafront, the crêpe stand, were they all still there, moving through the decades as I grew up? What of Madame Simkin, did I ever know her at all? Did she marry her Banyuls chap, had she been married before? I didn't know. Some of the changes to people, to life and to the town of Collioure transpired through Bette's letters, yet I could not see those alterations in my head.

The poet Machado, would he still lie under the heavy grey stone and brush-pines, silently receiving the daily visits of the young and not so young, drawn to his grave by the romance of his poetry? Of course he would, what tricks the memory plays. I kept them all as timeless entities. As I evolved they remained caught by my eye in 1967, as a photo is by the camera's lens: an instant, a moment, untouched and unchanged.

To my parents and Nico, I spoke very little, for they requested very little. The more time that elapsed of my three-month visit, the further from respective recognition and acknowledgement we grew. I most certainly had changed but to the people to whom you are related yet unmatched in terms of character and distant in terms of both proximity and personality, I was *'much the same.'* Even when I grew taller and experimented with a moustache they took me as *'much the same.'* My father used to look at me from the corner of his eye, as if he was trying to work out something new about me, something he hadn't noticed before. His face read back to me, *'nope, I just can't see it.'* This was the method he appeared to apply to life, from financial share figures to first-born son. My mother on the other hand, ruffled my hair and kissed me cheek to cheek, showing, what I thought was heart-felt affection. There was no denying the gesture. However I discovered she did it to everyone who walked through the house: the neighbours' two boys, the neighbour's cat, Great Aunt Peg, the neighbours' cousins. Her look of love passed right through you to the opposite side of the room, to a cupboard or chair which she subsequently dusted and re-organised after releasing you with an arm squeeze as if she'd been just about to do such a task until you stopped her train of thought for the automatic pleasantry.

One day, in the briefest of moments I speculated almost indulgently: *how had my parents ever come to conceive two boys?* Was there really a life, a love and a connection between these two people all those years ago? They were a mother and a father, categorised like any other, when had they ever been a Mary and a Robert? My father's current relationship with the present was impossible to fathom and my mother was in constant arrangement of the future. A ceaseless list of continuous occupations made her dart in and out of rooms. She kept the front door on the latch to visitors, the phone on and off the hook to callers; it was as if she was responsible for the spinning of Earth. It might rely on the daily pursuits of her and fellow moulds like her in order to function as it did, in ways we wouldn't understand because they (women) were misunderstood and we were self-important men. Jumble sales, cake sales, church-roof funding – when was the church roof ever *not* falling down; suffering from damp, peeling, rotting, leaking, seeping, leaning too far one way, housing birds, housing bats? It meant the past and those *'olden days'* were unchartered and unknown times, just as if you'd entered a soap opera only to realise it had been functioning years before you started, but you'd never caught up on those episodes, they'd been recorded over: gone, lost, done with.

As Nico aged he developed a sardonic grin which no-one seemed to notice but me. The grin grew in direct correlation to his annual income. Success of course, as he saw it, was measured in terms of how much money he pocketed. This achievement was the only thing my father *could* see. I then considered my own sense of goodness when I felt a tingle of joy at seeing my father's personal irritability at the favourable outcome and the ease of prosperity with which Nico was being lauded. At least I would not suffer envy, no-one in my family could be envious of Mothy Chambers. Nico would earn enough to buy off my father's secret resentment. My mother would feed and nourish him and Aunt Peg sat still with him. I would walk father down the garden path on visits and he'd pass away peacefully one ordinary day in his armchair having re-organised his book collection and having finished the last cigarette in the packet. Obligingly tidying up his study before exiting life. My mother seemed proud rather than upset, as if a touch of her fastidiousness had finally paid off.

Great Aunt Peg, a spinster from my mother's side, was a gentle and mischievous sort of person. She visited us when it pleased her and stayed during the spring and summer holidays for an ever-lengthening period of time. She had started this tradition from the time I was six months old. She had no experience of children but had a cheeky, childish manner of her own. We scooped frogspawn from the pond and kept it in a fish-tank, watching the metamorphosis of the little wrigglers into frogs. When they were fully grown we had frog races in the garden, encouraging the speckled green monsters to find their way back to the pond and not into mother's rose garden. We picked the caterpillars off the cabbages and made a home of twigs and leaves for them in warm jam-jars. When they became chrysalises, I moved the jars to the tree house and left the prospective butterflies to find freedom in the sunshine.

As age caught up on her, Aunt Peg picked up some peculiar habits. She believed there was a personal space existing between her and whoever tried to come close. This area was sacred; you did not enter it. As her girth expanded we were forced to stand some way back from her, which any onlooker would have perceived as odd: *'did she have a cold?' 'was she sick?'* It was easier to say *'yes'* than to explain her theory. She spoke quietly as if shuffling the words around her mouth but became capable of unpleasant shrill surprises. Her names for me from as early as I can remember to about 16 years included *'Timmy dear,' 'Timbo'* and *'Mothball,'* which she once screamed from the kitchen door and into our summer garden party. Then one sport's day at Rattle-snakes when I was 13 years and had made the finals of the sack-race, she joined the family day-out. You must understand luck was in my favour; there would be a red rosette for first place and Woof, the sportsman, had a stinging verruca. I was half way down the track, keeping between the white-sprayed lines and watching for dry, muddy stumps when I heard, amongst civilised claps and cheers, *'come on Timmy Tiptoes!'* She must have been saving her breath to expel what was exhaled as a giant bellow of embarrassment.

I was disqualified from the race for *'distraction to other competitors.'* An overweight Dick Cox took the red rosette, having been put in the race for *'sympathetic reasons'* - those being his grandfather had passed away, and he was set to inherit a fortune and several orchards in Sussex.

I spent the last week of term with a red face, grass stained legs and a head held extremely low. Naturally I suffered the consequences: humiliating jibes, smirks, innuendoes.

However, the luxury of the school's nine long weeks of summer holiday ensured the spirit of *'Timmy Tiptoes'* was exorcised from friends' memories. By the start of the winter term my 'sack-race name' was erased, for name-calling after an event that was 'historic' was considered unfunny.

Never again was Aunt Peg brought to sports-day. When she reached 90, everyone was labelled *'deary.'* With me it tended to be *'oh, deary me.'*

Bette sent letters, roughly four a year. With each letter I learnt a little more of her and of her life. There was still something special in all we shared and very literally something I could hold on to. It was only Woof and Lymy who heard about our correspondence. Ten years after my trip, in 1977, Woof found a moment to confront my musings.

"Bette this, Bette that, Philly's wife... what, are you in love with her Mothy?" Woof was blunt and sharp in one. He had an abruptness I could handle. After knowing and growing up with a friend you forgive certain characteristics, such characteristics you would not wish to find in new companions. Age and history would always lie on his side, even when we were parted for months, the old school ties and the catching up made our friendship stronger.

"No!" I said defensively. If someone strikes, you strike back: impulse, reflex, life's subconscious reaction. He was right though.

Love is a feeling not easy to define. It's different for everyone; it's incredibly complex and amazingly simple and this was that lifelong emotion, first love. Did I love Bette? I suppose so. The Bette I knew then, but who was she now? It was true, I had shamefully compared thereafter every girl's virtues to those of Bette. Thus, I had set my own dilemma and not one girl was favourable to my heart and mind. I had met with Jenny several times since 1967, but only, I sensed, when her beloved sister Gen, was out of the picture and even then, she could not help talking about her as if she was a physical part of her and if cut from thought, Jenny might not survive. I started to consider it slightly creepy. I could not think sensibly about Jenny and had to let her go.

"Perhaps you should try men?" Lymy had once blurted out. Woof and I were sitting on a grassy bank beside the River Avon. Lymy was leaning against a willow tree, blowing clear blue smoke rings into the air from an artistically-held, imported French cigarette. He detested crumpling his long trousers, preferring to stand as if modelling for a magazine shoot, convinced someone might spot his allure. Woof had his toes in the water, lazily chucking bits of stale white bread at disinterested swans.

"What's wrong with these bloody birds?" Woof presented an atypical impatience.

Lymy looked at Woof kindly; firmly and with a rather decorous air he removed the bag from Woof's irritated hand. *"Your technique's not right, first you have to shake the bag lightly, stand still and quietly, then come down to their level at the side of the bank... see like this,"* he demonstrated stylishly, ready to move from one static pose to another potential image shot, *"then toss a few pieces gently into the water, make a clicking sound. They can sense you're agitated... see... now they'll come."*

They hadn't come for Woof but they paddled over to Lymy who ended up feeding at least a dozen pure white, full-grown swans with six slices of bread. When the sun shone behind his figure and the rays fell either side of his silhouetted body, he appeared like a disciple of Christ, displaying an aura I thought once reserved only for Woof. This friend was also growing up differently, unexpectedly.

I would not fall in love with a man, but Lymy surprised me. He had a generous cut of femininity and it truly suited him. He had cultivated the air of an actor; carefully absorbing a variety of styles into parts of his life and finding the results rewarding. When he discovered something new to complement his image he need only be shown it once. He would perfect the role, mastering it far better than the original – leaving us only to wonder and admire. On our Stratford outing, with characteristic flair and impetuosity, he presented us with an instant recitation of a Shakespeare love sonnet adorned with an Irish lilt he'd picked up from a cousin. The tune floated rhythmically down the river on the back of one of his graceful swans, as if she might deliver the poem to the bank beside Holy Trinity Church.

So what were my more mature thoughts and feelings towards Bette? Perhaps to Woof or Lymy or anyone else who'd eavesdropped on our frequent chats, the answer would have been screamingly obvious, *'get in a car, drive to Collioure, see for yourself what Bette and all she encompasses, means to you... and take a friend to share in the adventure.'*

To wonder was one thing, to do something about your wondering was another. I spoke angrily to myself, *'don't be that complacent fool who did the talking but none of the doing. Don't spend 40 years regretting you didn't challenge yourself when the chance came.*

What was making me so reticent?'

When you are young, the war-time generation might push their unfulfilled ambitions your way. Disenchanted by the post-war period, they are left only with the vicarious pleasure of spending their later years living out their thwarted dreams through the experiences of the young and free. *"You should be happy not having to fight a war to save your country, freedom has been granted you... you take it as your right, for you know of nothing else but choice and liberty."*

Sadly, my parents could not raise the energy required to exert even the minimal amount of interest in my life. They remained in their remote, dusted world.

It was the logic and vigour of my two closest friends, with whom I shared my innermost thoughts, that lifted me out of my torpor and propelled me into action. The dynamic attitude and deep voice of Woof combined to put into action the Collioure reunion.

Lymy added his support, taking a break from his personal focus of attention to say, *"go where your heart takes you, my friend!"*

And so it happened. Together Woof and I would drive through France, taking his mother's Ford Fiesta, a small reliable car with a good number of miles already on the clock.

It was strange to now realise I'd not met Woof's mother or father, we rarely mentioned our parents. Unless someone had lost a relative early in life it was assumed you had the general set-up in place. It was not until Woof's memorial service that I met his two older, identical, twin sisters. I just didn't know of their existence and suddenly right there and then, at that awful hour I'd found myself wanting to fill the apparently wide gaps in the general knowledge of Woof. A chance lost in any of those easy, care-free, lazy times we'd squandered side by side. *'Why did I not know the simplest things about my best friend? What else would now be lost in death?'*

If I'd known how Woof's future was drawn I would not have hesitated or wasted a moment of time, but life is lived first and written later.

I scribbled an unusually rough and hasty letter to Bette, explaining my rash decision to come and visit. I said I'd be accompanied by my good erstwhile school-friend, the RAF pilot, Woof. I posted it four days before we left.

Woof, with granted leave status, picked me up early one June morning from my Keeper's Lodge beside the lake in St James Park in central London, aptly named Duck Cottage. The cottage was due new inhabitants and on return I would be finding more comfortable accommodation. Something, at least with running water and decent facilities.

The month began reasonably warm, there was a clear full-moon on the first, a good omen I affirmed. A few days later the weather turned cloudy and unsettled. The Queen's Silver Jubilee weekend celebrations were being prepared across the country, they made our drive a proud, delightful and partially-delayed jolly. In every village and town flew the Union Jack; red, white and blue bunting was strung from rooftop to rooftop and along lamp-posts. There were decorated motor vehicles for parades and long trestle tables set for street parties and festivals. I could taste the warm fizzy wine and the jam rolls and the burnt sausage baps and cake, always masses of good British cakes.

After making a slow course south, thirst and petrol made us stop at a pub, not far from the crossing point at the Port of Dover. At the suitably titled 'Britannia,' dressed in full jubilation and British glorification, final preparations were being put in place. Inside 'Billy' was adjusting a TV set in the corner. He was sweating profusely, the creases in his neck extending and contracting like a jack-in-the-box spring with grunts and slurs adding to the rhythm of his work. He was wisely left alone in a relatively hushed quarter, oblivious to the chaos and merriment taking place behind him. We gulped down two ciders served by a chirpy barmaid with a blonde perm and a slanted tiara who called everyone 'luv' or 'pet' when they entered and called out 'god bless yer' or 'cheers me dears' when they left. There was a great deal of activity and heightened expectation; we felt like intruders, like bystanders in a play about to be performed. Woof and I slipped out of a side door just as a loud *'hurrah'* sang from the lips of Billy. Time to move onwards, get across to France where none of this hullabaloo would be heard.

On the bumpy voyage across the Channel we established the best route to Collioure and on arrival at Calais, took to the roads immediately. Woof drove rapidly and, despite my insistence at stopping to rest and exchange drivers, he ploughed forth as if it had been a direct order from high command.

By 7pm I was ready for food and so, fortunately, was my chauffeur. Woof, always a man of sudden and exact decision swerved off the main road with the unindicated determination a Frenchman would have applauded. Within minutes we were approaching the outskirts of a mid-France small town, seeking rooms, sustenance and alcohol of no particular standard.

The name of the town began with *'N'* - the word was so long and we were so weary, we just named it *'Navi.'* The centre of Navi was formed of the traditional ancient square with a fountain playing. Several small children were chasing each other, occasionally dipping their hands into the water, splashing themselves and others, yelping and wailing. The sound bouncing off the old *'place'* stonework which had absorbed generations and centuries of cries. We spotted an ancient brick-built house which boasted a slightly battered and askew sign announcing *Auberge Christina*. Woof parked the Fiesta with great style and panache in front of our proposed night's accommodation with the confidence of a man who had pre-booked good rooms and assumed a welcome. Neither, as it happened, immediately materialised but with the charm of an undeniably handsome and hungry Englishman, Woof secured us two excellent rooms, the promise of breakfast and a recommendation of a local restaurant we could easily see on the other side of the square.

We were both young men, so time spent in our rooms prior to food and drink, was approximately five minutes. Long enough to relieve ourselves and wash minimally from our faces the many already processed miles.

From L'Auberge we loped languidly, hiding our somewhat desperate purpose, to the recommended restaurant. A table was instantly procured, the normally successful June season had not yet arrived here. It took us several seconds to decide on which beer to start our evening. As we allowed the refreshing cool, amber liquid to cleanse our palates we chose a bottle of the local cold, very dry white wine and, with the first temptation of our French arrival secured, we toasted each other, our trip and our futures and one last toast, proposed by Woof.

"To those we love and those we've yet to meet. May love remain eternal – for us all."

I matched his eloquent sentiment with one of my own, *"a toast to the future and a lifetime of good friends."*

We sat on our basket-weave chairs warmed by the early evening sun, our tiredness eased away; both in a quiet reverie of disbelief. *'Where were we?' 'How strange to have reached a town so perfectly at one with our mutual moods of expectation and youth.'*

We ate as only young men can and drank as only young men do. We exchanged stupid stories, we talked of superficialities, it was tired nonsense really. We didn't want to expand our friendship tonight other than to enjoy our freedom and our lack of commitments. Of tomorrow's drive, well, I left that to tomorrow's Woof.

Returning to our rooms we both collapsed on our hard, single beds and slept an over-indulged full night's sleep. Morning brought glorious sunshine, headaches and assorted stories of strange dreams. How odd, I thought, we should both have had muddled dreams. I blamed *la soupe de poisson*. We drank two very large, bitter coffees each and shared an enormous basket of relieving carbohydrates: the local boulangerie's croissants and baguettes, pots of red jam and a tub of melting sour French butter. We slathered the breads with butter, then added piles of sweet, lumpy jam, laughing together, but perhaps with separate thoughts.

"Better than that sludgy porridge and burnt-to-a-crisp-toast they used to call breakfast at Rattles-gate," Woof exclaimed with a blob of jam stuck to his cheek and crumbs in his mop of hair. For a split second there was the subtle confirmation of an absolute bond between us, an acquaintance that would last a lifetime and maybe more.

For me, the second day's drive brought forward the anxieties of this impromptu expedition into my past. For Woof, this was an escapade without rules or boundaries.

There was good light when we arrived in Collioure at about 8pm. There was a modern, newly painted hotel on the outskirts of the Old Town called Le Madeloc. I spoke in clear and confident French, attacking the words with verve and a little spit. One room was available for the first night and after tomorrow another would be free; we secured bed and breakfast for a week. It was the simplest plan affordable, although I could have happily swopped the next day's breakfast for a hot evening meal on the first night.

"Non, tis not possible."

My years of studying and practising French taught me one sure lesson, utilising a language was essential, or its fluency is certain to stagnate. Regardless of my assured approach, they spoke to me in broken English. I decided it was for their self-learning to respond so, rather than my own ignorance or poor-accented French. The overly-perfumed woman at the desk had thick-rimmed glasses and a sharp, slightly turned-up nose. If this Madame was to be painted you would have believed the nose had purposely grown upwards at the end to distance itself from the excessive dousing of cologne. Her pronunciation of English was extremely inadequate, and I felt oddly satisfied; a rush of linguistic triumph made me smile and consequently raised my face. I was healthier already. For the last leg we'd been feeding poorly, grabbing at a boulangerie late in the day or sharing a tin of meat and beans, anything cheap and portable. The one exception came towards the end of the journey when we pulled the car into a secluded copse and feasted on free-hanging pale-red cherries in the nearby field. Woof appeared as agile and adept at climbing the trees as the planes he flew, dipping, bending and circling the orchard for the ripest clump.

It was hopeless thinking I would sleep, and since Woof had covered the majority of the driving, I left him in peace for over an hour. I walked happily into town and wandered around the old *ville* to re-familiarise myself with Collioure once again. It was busy and warm. The stone walls and brick houses emitted the deep heat from an absorbed, intense summer sun. I could feel it brighten my pale English complexion. Compared to the brown tan and healthy glow of the Catalans, Woof and I were pallid, sickly *'erglishmen.'* Behind me, low in the sky, a parting gesture of joviality, hung a squiggle of soft pink cloud following the setting sun. Ahead of me rose a hillside of darkening greens and a vast bluey-white expanse of eastern sky, flattering the bay and reflecting the clear rocks shimmering in the saltwater. The Chateau, wrapped around the edge by the sea, exuded a wealthy, summer majesty, unlike the cold, harsh stone of winter with its spots of white sunlight. The secluded curve of sea was rested and calm. Baked to burning during the day, by evening the rocks released a comfortable warmth. Families lounged on the beach, sipping bottles of wine and snacking on baskets of food, complete in their comfort of informality. Small groups of children skimmed flat pebbles across the water, counting the bounces – *un, deux, trois* - as they grazed the surface and sank, others picked fat, heavy stones, plop, plop, plop, straight to the bottom. Were they making wishes as I had once done with Bette, with Philly and with Jenny? Ten years on, it still seemed a perfect little game: innocent, childish and dreamy. Somewhere in that little bay sat the rocks I had once thrown, with my hopes pinned to them, turning with the tide, some moving closer to the beach and others pushing deeper into the seabed. I thought I might see Philly, staring up at the sky, straining his neck and flapping instinctively like a wading bird, there was no-one of his personality amongst the cluster of people.

Chez Simone was open and so too was Les Templiers, both taking advantage of the seasonal temperatures. I cast a sideways glance towards Chez Simone, standing with my back against an extremely warm wall. There was a man who could easily have been an older Marcel, although in 1967, I had seen little of the chef. The tables and chairs on the exterior step of the restaurant were all taken, dessert pots and crumpled napkins indicating the end of a gently, gradated meal. I turned my head back to the bay and focused directly on the horizon, favouring a leftwards slant and allowed my ears to soak up the sounds without altering my angle. Squeals from an alcohol-warmed party, the clink of cutlery and plates, the screech of swallows, the mellow notes of an untraceable guitar-player: the sound-system of the summer air. The sharp cry from a baby diverted my head, I followed the call to Chez Simone. Simone sat on the dry-stone wall outside the restaurant with a burbling bundle, blowing air on its forehead to cool the woes. She took calming breaths in and out, settling the heated upset of the babe. Her method was simple and affective and I felt myself start to tire and yawn. I wondered if I was being observed while observing? I no longer wished to watch, I wanted to participate. By the time I walked past she had gone inside; the whole place appeared much smaller than I remembered.

Les Templiers also seemed slightly narrower. I had grown, no doubt, upwards to 6ft and lost all of my body's childish covering. Catching sight of myself in a mirror close to Les Templiers, my hair was shorter, the stubble on my chin was coarse and a thin line had formed down my left cheek. Wishing to make myself presentable for tomorrow's rendezvous with Bette and Philly became the impetus to force my tiring legs and feet forward, shifting them into an unwilling position and pace. I was keen to return to the hotel and gain some sleep in relative peace, comforted by the knowledge I had arrived in Collioure. Tomorrow I would re-awaken in that same place as artists, writers, poets and painters had done before me, using the magic and adding to the magic of this extraordinary town.

When I woke, a crack of light was streaming in through the thin curtains, teasing my eyelids. Woof had neatly made his bed and gone. Gone, but not far, only to the hotel's small garden of red and coral oleander bushes and several old olive trees where breakfast was served at a communal table. A small tray arrived when you took a spare seat, I was bleary-eyed and dozy and slightly unsure as to how things worked. *What was the correct etiquette for such a gathering?* Since the four other guests at the table, Woof included, had overcome the initial process of breakfast selections, I was critically regarded. It seemed I passed the test and everyone continued eating ravenously. No other guest followed me, so I did not have the opportunity to extend the same scrupulous analysis.

It was agreed Woof would accompany me to Bette and Philly's house on the Faubourg side, a ten-minute walk, maximum. If I needed time alone, Woof would make his excuses.

"You might like the church, Notre Dame des Anges or le cimetière, the cemetery behind the main square?" I said encouragingly.

"The one with the poet?" He asked and I nodded. So, during our drive he really *was* listening to all the words and reminiscences tumbling from my mouth as the French miles were consumed.

"Might check out that bar too... Les Templiers." He pronounced the name perfectly. His thirst for any undertaking and exploration was as much spiritual as it was physical. Woof spoke not as a traveller but as if he was coming home.

I knocked at Bette and Philly's small door, twice: 61, Rue de République. *How many times had I written that first line on a clean envelope?* I had imagined its journey, from my hand, through so many others, before reaching its recipient. I looked at the slender letterbox with its heavy flap and thought of my letters from England, dropping onto the floor: push, shuffle, slide. *"Looks like a letter from Mothy, Bette,"* Philly would call out, rearranging his glasses, stooping to pick it up and place it on her mantel-piece or into her hand. Bette had remarked, more recently, that Philly had begun to talk through his actions as if scripted, filling in the spaces normally left blank by processing the movements themselves.

Everything I remembered about Collioure would, from this moment forth, have to be adjusted and it would be difficult to sense what had changed: *was it me or was it the town?* I had indeed grown. My eyes on Bette had not changed one bit. She shone and sparkled, like a polished gem or a clean sea-pebble. The light seemed to be drawn to her and radiated from her, she appeared everso slightly more brightly lit than the rest of us, not unusually or strikingly so, just differently. In the same way one might spot a pretty young lady, the colour of her dress or twist of hair or the flirtatious expression, some mannerism or magnetism attracting the eye for longer than others who might pass without recognition or igniting interest. Bette wore a white chemise with ruffled cuffs and a long, light, fly-away pink skirt with a wide, bold belt. Her earrings and necklace of the same green stone glimmered in the light, maintaining an alluring sheen and lustre even when passing into the shade.

The 15-year age difference between us seemed reduced, almost non-existent, shrinking within minutes of meeting again. I had caught up at last. I remember the hug as a boy, now she kissed me cheek to cheek. Philly shook my hand and patted my arm with a lingering enthusiasm, giving him time to fully assess my change.

"Much taller, slimmed down a bit... thick, shaggy hair."

Philly was making his statement loud and clear with the scan of his glasses, summing me up physically with his three very pertinent comments. I introduced Woof, whom Bette had acknowledged already. It was only then I realised how casually well-presented and handsome Woof appeared in a neatly ironed, print shirt and fashionably long trousers. He was, after all, my guest and his worldly ways would surely reflect well on me but instead of pleasure I felt drab and dreary. I'd made an effort, yet it didn't seem so; standing beside Woof I appeared dull. I was another shadow to his reign. It was not a preoccupying subject only a late observation. I was quite happy and quite used to being eclipsed by others: Nico, Woof, Aunt Peg, our pet cat. It was only when I was alone with Bette I felt the benefit of her warmth, her encouragement and having someone care just about me.

A series of *'bon mots'* passed between us followed by a quick, practical catch up: the trip through France, our accommodation, and our plans. Then to change the subject and prevent an uneasy silence from breaking the evident pleasure of my arrival and of seeing Bette and Philly, Philly cried, *"fancy a crêpe you two?"*

"Oh no," said Bette, *"let's take the boys to Le Racou,"* Bette turned to me, *"Simone, you remember Simone? Her son is 18 months now, I told you about him. She mentioned there's a new bar down by the beach, it's a sandy shoreline... thought you might like to see it, I would!"* Bette showed great vim, although I really only wanted to keep to Collioure, any place either side of it would not contain the same reference points for me. Seeing Bette so animated and the thought of being an adult in her company

and avoiding the childish crêpe-stand option, a *"yes, alright"* popped straight from my mouth, with more vigour than I inwardly contained, already catching some of her infectious energy.

It was 7 minutes by car on the *corniche*. Crayon-green vines with their heart-shaped leaves grew in long straight lines along the stepped, stone terraces, striping the small undulating hillsides. At every curve was a rustic sign indicating the name of the producer *'Le Domaine Vieux,' 'Chateau Valmy,' 'Mas Hanicotte.'* Each *producteur* making claim to the superb wine of the Languedoc-Roussillon region. I mouthed them as we drove by. Woof was extremely talkative, sitting in the back with Bette: *"what a remarkable place," "what an interesting landscape," "what a fine climate," "what a special area to discover."* He was unstoppable. I felt like the parent, sitting in the front seat, ready to burst, ready to demand he *"pipe down"* like my father would do ineffectually to my brother and I. Yet another trait I'd remember to thank him for, better start a list. Yes, my mother would like that.

Through the window to the right was the deep blue of the Mediterranean. Several white sailing boats, fed by a light wind, were bobbing along gently on the calm surface, sleepy waves tapping and caressing their sides, their energy largely burnt-out by the sun. The Sun was God. Man and Nature were working in very relaxed, somewhat lazy harmony.

The granite rocks at the sheltered Catalan beach of Le Racou are where the Pyrenees dip their toes into the Mediterranean Sea. In truth, they are not officially the Pyrenees, they are a relatively smaller stepping-stone of the great range, known geographically as Les Albères. The village contains two or three basic, local shops, with no particular timetable. Small villas with overhanging fig and palm trees line one main, narrow street with narrower residential roads leading off. The inhabitants of Le Racou, having declared their independence from France in the 1960s, hold an edge of competitive rivalry between the neighbouring towns, believing themselves to be somewhat exclusive and individual – none of this seems to bother the other villages. The locals use the Catalan language to communicate between themselves and in the writing of road signs and street names, although in business they seem happy enough to succumb to a highly accented French. English visitors, treated with an amiable indifference, are left to fend for themselves.

Within the rocky and forested cove is a beach bar called *'Cerise.'* Woof and I chose cheap Spanish beers. Bette and Philly shared a rosé wine and we nibbled on almonds and sweet *croquants*. I couldn't quite believe we were together, after all these years and all the correspondence, I struggled to find my older voice or any suitable words. Write I could, to speak, well my throat was dry and my mind, without substance or coherence. *'Did I want to talk of the people and stories we had shared in letters? All that's been said, hasn't it?'* It was possible to repeat it, to go through it all again, bring it to life, face to face. So naturally we did. It seemed sensible, and, for the sake of Woof, we briefly explained each person when their time came.

Claudie, now reaching 95 years of age, was no longer

taking visitors, *"not even Bette,"* Philly emphasised. Tony was now working a part-time shift; he'd been promoted and was making more money now than he did on a full week's work. It was still hard, manual labour, he was not a bookkeeper or office-man, but he did have the stamina and strength younger men lacked. Many of the town's boys were extending their education, searching for smarter yet sedentary positions. The bigger cities and higher wages provided the incentive. Long, labour-intensive, injurious hours were the push. *"Desk and pen lads,"* Tony had said of them or some such equivalent. Very little impressed Tony, *"except Bette,"* Philly had emphasised, proudly. Bette and Tony met at the Sunday market, Bette exchanged a homemade jam or cake or pie for a weekly snippet of information on Claudie's health and well-being. In the last few months Claudie had flicked meticulously through her photo albums, making short notes and dates under each of the frames and affixing them securely to the dark leaves of her collection. She drank a large coffee with cream, ate a small diet of baguette, topped with *un fromage du chevre* and slithers of salted tomato, sometimes a sweet tart and always a glass of reddish-brown *banyuls* before closing her bedroom shutter and whispering a prayer to the wind, a thank-you to the birds and bidding a good night to the bats, to anything that could fly, *'send word.'*

Marcel, the chef at Chez Simone, was running a good kitchen; he'd become redder, fatter and friendlier. The business had blossomed. It was well-known the key summer months were crucial to local enterprises and traders. The money made then would cover low periods across the winter or bouts of unpredictable, off-season weather which, especially around June, was still a possibility. Waiter Jacques had moved on further North, reputedly heading to Paris. He'd spoken to Bette about the dream of running his own restaurant in London, a French one of course. *"I always encourage dreams,"* Bette had said.

Simone and her little tot, Julian, lived adjacent to Bette and Philly, having moved from above the restaurant to the Faubourg neighbourhood. There *"various parents take turns watching over each other's children playing on the nearby beach or in and out of houses and down lanes."* It was a much better option for her.

"We're very close, like an extended family," Bette had said, smiling reflectively.

While we were talking Bette looked at me and across at Woof and very sweetly asked about me, my family and friends, *'those I had talked and written about so vividly.'* She'd often felt she could see and admire them just as I had described. One day, if they came calling and sat round her table she would instantly love and know each one as if they'd been friends all their lives. Woof had liked the sentiment. Philly remained mostly quiet, listening with appropriate but muted interest. He was seeking something else, his eyebrows twitching, his glasses in his breast pocket moving up and down with the air in his lungs, his fingers tapping soundlessly to an imaginary tempo. Was it the sky, the light and shade? The slender fall of rock stretching like a giant's foot into the sea-water bay? Was it a vegetable he'd missed at the market? He wouldn't be able to cook up the traditional version of ratatouille, and they had guests. If the clouds, as forecast, obscured tonight's sky he'd have to forego a clear vision of summer stars. His mind was silently busy and alive, questioning all tricks: a trick of the eye, a trick of the senses. I was aware of wearing a puzzled expression, mirroring Philly: *'stars, weather, stew.'* His three words to summarise those internal musings. Keep it short, remember it for longer.

I was still trying to comprehend my situation. I'd grown up physically but my emotions surrounding Bette and this area remained those of my childhood and, as such, confused. I longed for her to keep talking or else risk a jibe from Woof about *'love and being smitten.'* I was certainly on my guard, for whatever embarrassing quip he might think up. How my mind was a maze of many routes and few endings. As Bette released information I seemed to fill with a knotted anxiety. I was *'nervous fizz in a bottle of pop,'* Nico had once said of me. Nico only need observe people once before deciding what they were like and what category of his organised brain he might place them under, if they were worth the bother. I was family so to observe me was of no further value to him. We were definitely different.

"What about Madame Simkin, Bette," I asked with affection. *"How is she fairing?"* I did hold a genuine interest in my old French teacher, more so than those teachers at Rattles-gate.

My mind strayed back to the couple of old-boy school reunions I'd attended. Woof had chosen to suffer three in a row. I include Woof's acts since he is woven into this part of the tale, *my* doings are not the only ones to absorb. The social gatherings had been peculiar, dis-connected evenings. I fought the butterflies in my stomach, the scent of school wood-polish, the odour of boiled potatoes and the smell of fear when the bells rang. When I shut my eyes a set of forthcoming exams loomed overhead. My former teachers were older and rather tired, age had given them a dull complacency. They needed a fresh flow of blood to stimulate their grey faces. I remembered none of the pupils from previous years and spent the evening with Woof and Lymy, as I did most of the time anyway. The three of us felt disinclined to engage with the other men from school, despite the freedom to pick and choose friends without the segregation of age or academic ability. We wandered the school halls, read the neat work on the classroom walls which I found, with great satisfaction, was hung too low to read, and drank glasses of flat Spanish wine at the side of the sports field. We were allowed to break the rules, so we did and made unsuitable, silly comments. A well-dressed and respectable-looking Dick Cox had made a brief entrance and exit. Lymy claimed to have scared him off using his *"frisky, blithesome, gay ways."* He had combined three of his favourite words of the moment. I admit his tactics were extremely indiscreet, but between us it became something of a joke. The more wine Lymy drank, and with nothing to absorb it, the more flamboyant and outrageous he was, mostly because he'd secretly wanted to perform this for years, so did. He wasn't invited back, but I don't think he cared, he'd made his all-boys, public-school statement.

Returning to the subject of Madame Simkin, Bette relayed the news that only the other day she'd received a postcard from her. She had taken passage to Martinique with her Banyuls chap about a year back. This was something I had remembered from a long letter at Christmas. The card and a short scribble was the first notice of their safe arrival. She had not marked the date so it was unclear when they had made port or where they were headed. So it was assumed they were on the well-sheltered Caribbean side of the Island; the weather was tropically warm and the flora and fauna were exquisite. Madame Simkin had given up her teaching role and connection to English school parties when her dog Paul had died. *"She never entered a classroom again,"* Bette said soulfully.

"We met her man, Clement... several times... after she lost Paul. Very charming, very sincere, he was. Quite an adventurer... owned a sleek sailing boat. I think he was reputed to have taken part in the Olympics... once upon a time. She was very happy, that's what was important. She gave Philly a big kiss goodbye!" Bette looked the way of Philly. He lifted his eyebrows, nodded and smiled widely. He blushed red and waved his hand back and forth, *"she did it to everyone!"*

"We miss her and think about her... it was good to hear she was safe... finding a new life in a new place." Bette stopped abruptly, she looked weepy. The wine had fuelled emotion into some of her fast-moving thoughts, reminiscing was indeed a tiring affair.

Woof offered to accompany Bette on a stroll down to the nearest pool of water to cool her feet. She agreed, *"it would refresh my senses, in the way wine relaxes them."*

If Philly could not see Bette required air and movement then it should have been me who tended Bette. Here was a third person, Woof, he'd not been in our French-family picture before and now here he was, considering Bette and realising Bette's needs and she accepted them when I thought she'd have feigned an independence or shown her usual self-sufficiency.

I needed to readjust my picture of this place. I couldn't think straight, there were too many people involved, they were crowding me and clouding my judgement. They were dancing in and out of my vision, first in the way I remembered them and second as new individuals.

Later, Woof and I went to supper at Philly and Bette's. It was an unappetising event, my taste-buds jaundiced, but Woof relished the meal. Roast chicken and burnt gratin potatoes followed by a cherry *clafoutis* full of stones with crème fraiche. Bette and Woof chatted amiably, once or twice she glanced at me. I know because I seldom took my eyes off her. She was like a hot flickering fire in winter: hypnotising and absorbing, or a pool of fresh water in summer: a source of much-needed pleasure. I did not blame Woof for his admiration and closeness to Bette, but I did not have to like it. Philly was used to the attentions Bette received, he was not a jealous man. What a begrudging face I must have worn; the painful, frustrating and all-consuming trait that is jealousy.

Philly was up and down to the kitchen. I offered to

help and he jumped at the suggestion. I was certain he'd say no, thank me for the polite gesture and carry on with the messy task he had set himself. I was wrong about him too. So Philly and I busied ourselves, serving charred chicken and crispy thin potatoes, then thick-skinned cherries dotted in a light sponge and a slightly sour crème fraiche. I pardoned myself soon after, bluffing a weak stomach and fatigue, and unsurprisingly, both came true.

I took a walk along the edge of the chateau wall into town. The seafront and main cobbled alleys were lit by large, bulbous, twin-lighted lampposts. A cry of laughter and chink of glasses broke my self-immersion and my feet took their direction from the sound. The only place open to a late flow of vain, forlorn and world-weary beings, where I might console my baffled soul and pick up some rugged French habits: Les Templiers.

Outside many guests were finishing their evenings under the white and blue awning I'd sat beneath as a student. I wondered where Hannah might be now, could she be one of these hefty, solid, chain-smoking women, their hands not far from a glass of wine and a cheese knife slicing through a tasting plate. I went inside where several single men sat at tables for two, and two tables of four played a quiet hand of cards. I positioned myself right at the back, into the dark wooden corner. There was a healthy cigarette still burning at a nearby empty table, I picked it up and let the ready-lit tobacco stain my fingers and burn my nose and throat. I hadn't smoked a good cigarette in a long while, and since it was sitting there I did us both the favour. I was feeling low and listless and probably mildly depressed. I was not sure what I'd expected of this visit but I'd never intended to find my soul as gloomy as this and no musical blues to fill the empty recesses of my heart.

A man, of average build to me, with black hair flecked with grey, a grey-tinged itchy beard, and sunburnt, gnarled hands, sat two tables away. He appeared to feel the same pains and to lament the same woes. Perhaps he held a far greater personal hardship, but how does that help you with your own sadness? It doesn't, for you are too absorbed by your own concerns to ponder too long the pains of others. Clearly, I was in 'good' doleful, sombre company: *'out-of-sorts hommes, this end of the bar.'* Those who find themselves *'down in the doldrums,'* trapped like a sailboat without wind, caught and unable to move, only to bide time, must sit and wait the inevitable consequences.

Bette and Woof were, in such a short time, undeniably close. They had instantly struck-up a friendship and familiarity I was surprised to see. I mulled it over too much until it pained like an ulcer on the tongue. Once I'd seen this closeness, I could see nothing else and Woof held nothing back. *'A gentleman, a charmer, a ladies-man,'* my three ways to sum up his overseas character.

I ordered two glasses of Muscadet and a carafe of red and then a sweet banyuls (with this I toasted Claudie). At first, I thought I might fool the barmaid into thinking I was expecting company but she'd seen this ploy before, especially as a solitary hour passed and I made my way through the contents. I discovered I had quite the taste for it and it seemed to soften the blows to my heart as my mind continued to play over the apparent affection and mutual intuitiveness between Bette and Woof. Philly had his head in the clouds, the stars, the moon, something celestial: unreachable and unfathomable. Why did he not feel my angst? Was this such a regular event to him?

On the barque bar was a soft pencil and in my pocket a small clear notebook. Feeling unable to make sense of a worsening situation the more inebriated I became, I decided to sketch my table assortment of drinks. An earthenware jug, a wide chipped glass, an ashtray and stub, a short, thick glass, a few olives and olive stones, a few sheets of plain paper, I was not displeased with the results. I gazed at the colourful paintings hung on the walls exactly as they had been 10 years ago. Pastels, watercolours, oils, chalks, some new acquisitions, some, newly positioned. My piece would not warrant a room for the night in lieu of payment but it summarised my unenviable evening. I signed the drawing and left it with the barmaid as she chatted to a man dressed entirely in black.

"Pour la collection d'art," I said, pointing to the walls and catching the smug look of Picasso from his set-piece photo, eyeing up my failings, making a list with his thick, brown free-flowing talented fingers and then throwing it back at me with his deep eyes. He was still the revered, unchanged genius.

I was about to make my way outside as a storm threatened to break. The brooding and rumbling began and then a roar of thunder so arresting it cracked the belly of the black sky. To be trapped by the illness of thoughts was my own inescapable doing, to be trapped by an impending downpour was something I refused to allow. I escaped. It was an achievable task. The wind had changed course. The plane tree leaves were flying wildly above and whipping and snapping at the branches. An electric current cut across the sky and flashes of lightning lit the bay and hillsides. My walk uphill would have to be quick, although my chest felt weak and my knees felt locked and ungreased.

However, the next 7-minute stroll to Hotel Madeloc was both long enough to avoid the rain that later came lashing and, most important of all, it was something quite Biblical. Was it laid out for me? Possibly. In less than 10 minutes I witnessed a complete change of vision in Collioure. I saw a crouched, young, African boy with a cap beside him, *"faim et sans abri"* he called out and again as I fumbled for change, *"faim et sans abri."* Hungry and homeless. His foot was bandaged with makeshift cloth and his right hand was deformed. Further up the street, in the middle of an uneasy quiet road, lay a dying bird, knocked carelessly by a car. The life fluttering out of its little shocked body; the feathers perfectly soft, its unique markings fading as its travels dissolved into the earth. No longer was it important to preen and polish his full-grown dress.

As I made my turn towards the Hotel with its night sign alight, another young man came searching from the direction of the station. He was scruffy with heavy eyes and sunken cheeks, and had a red, scabby cut on his forehead and chin. He too wanted money, *"mes affaires ont été volées."* His belongings had been stolen. *"Seulement ce soir."* This evening. I handed him a crushed packet of three cigarettes, a box of matches marked 'The Anchor Inn' and a handkerchief with my initials, TC. Woof had slipped the cigarettes into my jacket that afternoon, declaring, *'I'm quitting the stuff.'* So it seemed that as Woof improved himself I descended into a world of intoxicating bad habits: drink, cigarettes and self-indulgent melancholy.

What exactly was the purpose of this 'Biblical walk?' I had never witnessed these *'sorts of characters'* in Collioure before (I make reference to Aunt Peg's definition of these men from her weekly sojourns into London). Did I need to be shown the sad sufferings and plight of others, to bear witness to the fears and issues I did not have? Must I acquiesce to how profoundly fortunate I am? How very lucky was I *not* to have to consider any of these frightening misfortunes in my life? My life was my own and my future held a multitude of possibilities.

I pulled the late-night bell and after 5 minutes, the sky growling, my heart panting and my knees locked tight, Madame Madeloc, grudgingly opened the thrice-bolted hotel door. As I entered the heavens opened and torrents of rain poured down and into drains, sucked into the ground, anywhere it could find to escape. What about the brown boy, the station man, the dainty, dying bird? By morning they would be washed away. I wouldn't see them again, but I *had* seen them, the night of a June thunderstorm; they were alive in meaning and as clear as day. Bette had probably seen them once, she could see everything.

Part XI – II

A sharp, hot ray of white sun bleached my pillow; I hadn't pulled the shutters to. The whole window was full of bright light; the single ray caught my eye. A message from the sun to wake and rise. It was nearly midday. I'd easily missed breakfast; my throat was dry and my stomach complained. My whole body seemed angry with me. My eyes were sore and red, my shoulders felt tense. When I turned my head to the right the muscles pulled, they tightened and throbbed. I'd slept heavily on my left hand, which, feeling insulted, produced a painful cramp, lasting a long three minutes. A cold shower was not what I wanted but what I would need to face the day

There was a note pushed carefully under my door. Hastily written with a pen whose ink was scratchy. I read a short message of both invitation and command.

"Come to Chez Simone at 10.30am. Woof."

My first reaction was not kind. *"Yes Woof, whatever you say, I mean you're the reason I came, I'll just follow you like a pilot fish."*

Then I thought sensibly, *'wherever Woof is, Bette is sure to be. Damn-it, I'm late... I'll see Simone and she'll tell me what to do. I can work with instruction... it's fumbling about with these feelings that makes me so low.'*

After thinking rationally, I fell back onto a thought I'd

considered more than twice: *'Why did I take this trip with Woof and not Lymy? I'd have had none of this troubling envy.'* I answered myself always the same way, *'the idea had been Woof's so it's only reasonable he should have come. And besides, between the three of us, discounting Olly who was more distant, Woof and I were the better friends. Lymy was extravagant and entertaining but slowly moving away into a new crowd who shared his passions and flair.'*

I left Madame Madeloc (sitting sleepily at front reception) to increase the permanent deep frown in her forehead and her championship look of disapproval as she watched me through heavy, lowered lids, fumble with the door and leave.

I walked as speedily as I could, the town was filling fast with tourists, day-trippers and dawdlers. I darted between children and their melting ice-creams, gasped at the penetrating smell of fried fish, and as I passed Les Templiers a flash of last night's stupor caught my conscience with a little guilt. It was odd to see by day my place of refuge washed clean of the previous night. The open interior, its customary cool, dark brown, passed no judgement and now played host to a fresh coterie of coffee-drinkers.

During the entire week, Woof did not make it inside Les Templiers. I was secretly pleased. This one place where I had once sat happily as a young, naïve boy with Bette and Philly and now frequented for its Muscadet, would not be inspected and taken over by him. Although towards the end of the week Bette remarked, *"it'll be something for you to come back for."*

My ears pricked up, dispatching a direct note to brain, *'yes - Les Templiers - make it the perfect excuse to come back Woof, when really you wish to see more of Bette. It'll be me at the bar talking to Picasso's photograph and you two on the beach.'*

I met Simone with a friendly hug and we chatted, standing under the shade of the restaurant canopy.

"You have grown." She began.

"Yes." I responded automatically.

"You look tired."

"Yes."

"You're here with a friend... Woof?"

"Yes... No, the friend is here with me." She understood the difference straight away.

Then we reversed.

"How is little Julian?"

"Tired... growing fast... keeping me on my toes." She liked this particular idiom and to make three succinct observations, a habit of Philly's too.

"How's business?"

"Very good... especially this time of year. Marcel is here, Jacques left."

"Oh yes, I heard."

Then followed a hustle as arriving clients jostled for free tables. Simone refocused and recognising my anxiety told me what I should have guessed.

"Bette and Woof have gone. They waited for you. Bette was worried and wanted to phone, but the wires are down... you know after last night's heavy rain. They've taken a walk to Le Moulin, up through the stepped olive groves." She rolled her eyes and shrugged her shoulders. Clearly the storm had brought about other irritations but I need only know the part that affected me.

"Oh right... I had a late-night and... when do you...?"

"They'll be back around one. Have a drink Mothy. It's not as hot today. The thunderstorm cleared the air but the temperatures'll go up again, probably into the 30s. Oh yes, too hot for me, too hot for most." She fanned herself with a paper menu.

"See that couple... out by the rocks, in the white hats... there." Simone pointed to the active bay with bobbing bodies and toy-boats, *"they swim everyday... up to the side of the clocher and then back to the line of rocks. They must be in their late 70s. Brave and resilient the people of Collioure. They've seen a lot and make the most of what they have."*

Simone let me ponder her words. She nipped to the back of the bar, then returned, deftly handing me a tiny black coffee, *"café fort,"* she said. I took a sip, it was bitter. I concluded there and then, the most disgusting tastes can do some good. Some of life's temptations are both terribly bad and terribly satisfying, depending on who you're with and where you are in body and in state of mind. I heard a piercing baby yell from inside the bar area. Simone spun round, disappearing as if a pile of saucepans had clattered to the floor.

"Hullo Mothy." I turned to see Marcel. He'd popped out of a sweaty kitchen to replace Simone's absence and to speak English. *"Bette et Simone is teaching me English... how... are... you...?"* He spoke very clearly. *"Do... you... need... a cigarette? The weather is... beau."*

"Marcel! I'm fine... well... good." I was picking at words he might know: the magic three. He was following my mouth and his hairy ears twitched happily. Yes, he could understand all this.

"Yes, do you have a spare cigarette... an extra one...?"

He was not as scary as I remembered. A brown burnished face, he'd shaved his moustache for the summer; his hair was thinning, his waist-band widening and his personality had broadened. He was content being employed in the small town over the summer and thrived under pressure of heat and of mood. As long as a cigarette could be sucked, red-meat could be chewed and sea-air inhaled all was well.

He polished his spectacles. I'd grown up, he'd grown out and we shared a cigarette moment, just as you might with a stranger in an English pub garden. We lit up in each other's company only for a few minutes, but in retrospect it was a warm, effective few minutes. In the smoky air, nothing much was said in words of any language but there hung a feeling of general, manly comfort. It was enough. My thoughts began to trail elsewhere and with a small shock Marcel exclaimed the two names at the forefront of my introspection.

"Bette et Woof... there!" Marcel said, pointing a podgy garlic-scented finger into the air and then repositioning my head. *"Où?"* I said in thrusting French, but I'd already located them.

Up on the furthest hillside, within Collioure, were the silhouetted frames of Bette and Woof. I traced their contours as they steadily made their way down through the contorted olive groves to the sheltered museum garden. It was too late, I had lost the chance to join them.

Bette wore a long flapping skirt and a wide summer hat, one hand kept the hat in place, probably her left because she was right-handed, while the other arm was stretched to the side. Woof was helping her make the steps downhill. Le Moulin was newly dressed for June-milling and a slight breeze was turning the white sails.

Ten years ago I had sat on a cold, mossy pew under a silvery green eucalyptus tree waiting in the museum's shadow for Philly. I had peeled strips of the bark from the shredding trunk and watched startled ants scurrying tirelessly up and down and around the soft wood: little workers in their jobs for life. The overgrown oasis was unchanged by years. At its centre a stone fountain of three cherubs supported a scallop dish of gently dropping rainwater; a place so full of tranquillity. I remember absorbing its peace and settling my worries; these worries I have now forgotten. The creeper-covered brickwork seemed to have blocked out the modern world as it continued to grow an untidy secret garden, touched only by seasonal scents from sun-heated leaf oils to a sweet autumn maturity.

I watched as Woof strolled indifferently through its stillness. My eyes were exceptionally clear and sharp. I shivered with surprise and alarm as if he had chosen to purposely trample on my past. Woof was my lifelong friend; there was nothing mean or deliberately hurtful about him. All he had done, he had done without malice or forethought, but the damage had been done. The day fell cold. My memory felt robbed by the present.

Marcel brought me out of my daydream.

"Bette, she's not look as bright as normal... probably the summer sun very high ... she and Woof look the same." He put out his cigarette and went into the kitchen, Simone was calling him away, there were meals to prepare.

So Marcel observed something too. Bette always appeared a touch more luminous next to other people, with the exception of Simone, but they had a long-held, precious friendship and obviously some of Bette's shine was in Simone as well.

Bette and Woof shared a spiritual closeness I knew I did not possess and I felt genuinely disappointed: why had I not been given it? Between Bette and Philly there was love and friendship, care and compassion. I felt like the extra child in the family, just as I had been at home. I had never fully understood where I fitted in or what to do with what I had. I could write letters but I couldn't connect on the higher plain. Where does that sphere lie? Between the Earth and the Moon? The Earth and the Sun? Wherever it is I am not equal to it.

The second half of the week became even more tiresome and demoralising for me. The weather grew hotter which was trying for any British complexion and for any control of sensibilities, even the previous long summer of 1976 could not prepare me for the heat of the Mediterranean. The nights were stifling. Lying between the hard, hotel sheets (as hard as Madame Madeloc's glare when I asked if breakfast would be the same choice everyday) I waited for the temperatures to fall so I might eventually cast off into sleep-land (old mother-matron's words which Woof occasionally used in his parlance). I struggled to get three, maybe four hours a night.

Each evening Philly insisted we gather on the rocks by the harbour arm for a spectacular June sunset. According to his many years of experience this was the best month for glorious displays of Catalan orange, vermillion red and volcanic pink.

"Many painters use the knowledge of these celestial colours of the South in their work."

The sky was uncluttered by clouds; the sun undeterred by the daily need to pass its warmth and light to a waiting world. The afterglow softened sculptural corners; the rose light and warm shifts of air melted into the cracks and crevices of stone and terracotta. This is what made the Mediterranean life grow. Being so warm (I thought too hot) made the occasion relaxing and energising in one. The best part of the day, was the ending of it.

The 8ᵗʰ June was a Wednesday and a new summer market day. Philly was up at dawn buying boxes of apricots, peaches and nectarines. It was the start of their much-anticipated season. There had been talk of a destructive moth and an intensely-prolonged drought. No-one was sure how abundant the crop would be and Philly wanted to make an apricot preserve before Woof and I returned home. He caught me at about 8am, making my way to Les Templiers, *'for a different kind of breakfast.'* Actually, that day he rescued me. I helped him home with his load and *he* restored my faith in the three of us. What we had truly shared those ten years ago would remain unforgotten and untouched. I sat at the old kitchen table with Bette and Philly. Bette made a pot of strong, English tea and we talked with a reserved familiarity. I wandered around the house, there were still boxes on the stairs, my room no longer had a desk and the pots of herbs were full of rosemary and thyme. Bette's mantelpiece still held her precious items. Through the open, top window, I could hear the train chuff, roll, heave and whistle. The morning scent of baked butter pastries and burnt sugar was beginning to ooze through the walls. The deep, sweet tarts would be sold *'after lunch when the crème anglaise had set and the fruit was puréed and sliced and then finished with a glaze of apricot jelly.'* Bette knew. We looked at one another and smiled. We all felt the same thing, *'how delicious, how tasty, how good to be here.'* I stayed for another tea. This time happier, more relaxed and relieved: my three words. Philly set to work on his apricot conserve, cutting the apricots from *'full-moons into half-moons into quarter-moons.'* Bette saw me to the door. Philly came out. He had sugar on his glasses and coral-coloured fingers. *"It's the third-quarter phase of the moon today, eight days before a new moon... we'll catch it later! Well, we can't catch it... we'll see it!"*

Bette's eyes sparkled and her jewellery glittered. I did love her. She and Philly were a perfect couple, together in Collioure, this special Catalan town. It discovered, and was discovered by, many unusual and exceptional people. Living a life such as this: apricots, sunsets, moon-phases, painters, markets, good wines and sea-air. A whole different world?

Had the evening been our last, it would have been the finest way to end my stay. We were booked for another three. I recall only one. Suffice to say I kept a cosy seat corner warm in Les Templiers and ventured out in the evening at the insistence of Philly to stare at the sky and *'its many miracles.'* I saw Woof each day with Bette or Simone or both. Philly kept watch over Julian very occasionally and was frantically preparing events and overseeing the summer schedule at Le Centre Culturel. He was trying to co-ordinate the arrival and stay of a jazz band from New Orleans. It was potentially an exchange mission: jazz from the Deep South, for *'the musical marvel, Jean-Pierre Sola, pianist extraordinaire.'* The Americans were going to need some strong convincing. Philly, with his ways of seeing the world, felt he was the best man for the task.

The one surreal evening I do remember was a specific highlight in the summer programme of Collioure. Five brightly painted old fishing boats were harboured close to the Chateau, seesawing gently, up and down on a mild wake. The tall wooden sail-poles with white-sails wrapped tight were covered in a bunting of Catalan flags: four red stripes on a yellow background. Some fisherwomen were tidying their husband's nets and humming and singing their warm, end-of-day songs. *"Lullabies to the sea for bringing their men home safe... sometimes the late moon and stars guide them, or an early dawn."* Bette had said.

At 8.30pm a yellow and blue boat set sail to the tune of an eleven-man band. One man steered the quiet, motorboat while three others tied lanterns, fixed tangled flags and then settled for position. The old boat, spruced and mended, looked hard and uncomfortable. The scene was the idealised dream of the Mediterranean. On shore two circles of dancers, about ten in each circle, were holding hands. The ladies wore long white skirts with a head-covering similar to a tea-towel and the men wore long black trousers some with a red sash. With small, light steps they began *'la sardane,'* the traditional dance of Catalonia. The rhythm of the wind instruments caught a mood of absolute joy and harmony. At 9pm the clocher struck its nine evening chimes and the coloured lanterns on the fishing boat were lit with candles; they dangled like illuminated beehives. Half an hour later, on the beach, a huge organised bonfire, piled high with pine branches, was set alight, crackling with fury and blazing fiercely. We were all hypnotised by its white, burning heat. Bette dazzled: her face, her jewellery. She had a captivating glow. Woof and I both caught each other staring at her. I'm certain he read jealousy in my face. He stepped back, not in motion but in thought, and diverted his eyes back to the fire, letting his emotions burn-out in the ashes. I knew we would not talk together of Bette or any of this Collioure week. It was safer to keep words inside the head, to think them, but not to utter them. We were men, that would be easy. With women, I had seen fireworks follow a disagreement, a misunderstanding, a spite; it was unhealthy, it was destructive. He would not keep correspondence with Bette. Bette knew writing would be our connection. Woof and she had found something else, that *'higher plain,'* I thought.

After a rather hushed period between the four of us, Philly explained the display taking place. *"The 23rd of June is Fete Saint-Jean. Tonight's a practise run... they'll be more people in two weeks."*

"D'you mean Joan of Arc?" Woof asked.

"No, no Saint John... the Baptist. Some write J.O.A.N some J.E.A.N. The celebration takes place on the eve of his feast day, at sunset on the 23rd of June. He was born six months before Christ... so we commemorate the night before the anniversary of his birth on the 24th. It's a happy occasion... an honouring of the birth rather than the death... as is the case with so many Saints. High spirits, jubilant, blessed!" Philly articulated.

"Thank you for the lesson," Woof smiled and I agreed,

"I'd never have known."

"Of course, Bette and I particularly love this festival... it coincides with the Summer Solstice, give or take a day... the longest day of the year... a celebratory time for all!"

Bette sighed a whispered *"yes"* in agreement. The flames from the fire reflected on Philly's glasses, his eyes were fixed on Bette. What could I read, in my inexperienced mid-twenties? He loved her completely although he knew he did not completely understand her.

The three quarters moon was high and waning. The sky was intensely black. A scattering of stars twinkled and blinked; a mass reaching far back into infinite space, speckled with one silvery gem and millions of crumbled crystals. The moon-cycle for the month was being rubbed out little by little, day by day, before a new moon arrived. The date, for the next full moon was the 1st July and one on the 30th July. This made, *"two in one month... and you know what that means?"* spoke an excitable Philly.

"A blue moon month!" We all three sang and laughed.

The look on Philly's face was priceless, as if his lessons had been finally absorbed by his pupils. I know Woof and I were thinking of our old school days: *'knowledge, learning, discipline.'* Gosh we already went back quite a long way and our friendship would weather whatever, or so I thought.

Part XII

It took us two days to get home and for me, over two weeks to recover. Woof returned to duty, this time to an airfield amidst the flatter pastures of Somerset, and promised to send word of our next meet-up date and location. I had caught some dreadful bug, most likely following our exhausting drive and a disastrous meal. We made a misplaced holiday-saving at a budget hotel masquerading as an auberge of style on the outskirts of Calais. I was confined to a dark bedroom and three-day diet of warm water, sugar and salt, to starve it out. This I did back home with my parents, where life was simple and unchallenging. I was currently homeless awaiting the summons of work and workplace.

I received a card from Woof a fortnight later, which I struggled to read. He had scrawled, as my eyes saw it, his new address and the name and address of a pub, 'The Dolphin Inn', plus a date to get together. I was feeble and weak, and tendered my excuses. The middle distance between us seemed a stretch too far. Having just recovered from the illness I needed to begin the process of gradually building myself up again. So I did. Firstly, with porridge, made with water and salt, and dry biscuits; then potatoes from the garden allotment, done every which way, and strips of cooked, cold-meat inside plain bread. Thereafter I was not able to resume a liking for vinegar or whole-cooked, un-fileted fish that stared back at you on the plate (this disappointed Aunt Peg who placed weekly orders for fish from Cornwall to be delivered to the house every

Friday she stayed with us). She was not staying, she was living, and in many ways she was helpful with father as chatty companion and chess-player. Mother was fully occupied with her incompletable set of jobs. I think she felt she'd done her time with him: caring, supporting, nurturing. If she didn't find pursuits and hobbies of her own she'd be locked into his gloomy cloud. Aunt Peg couldn't see what mother saw, so acted as the rainbow between the two of them, back and forth like a perfect arc and always dressed in too many bright and clashing colours. I spent many days stumbling about, finding my feet and strengthening not only my appetite but my body and senses. I kept sunglasses on, avoiding Aunt Peg's vivid daywear, and stayed predominantly indoors.

After four weeks at home, much rested and rejuvenated, I was sent the address of my next lodging: a small rectory in the weald of Kent. It was here, several months later, I heard news of my father's death. I returned home for a week to show my face and, if allowed, to help with matters.

The funeral took place in the local church, All Saints. I decided to pass on the whole-fish and chips with vinegar style send-off, Aunt Peg had arranged. I did stay for drinks with distant cousins, who failed to see a single change in me. I could hear the echo of their thoughts, *'nope, just can't see it... hasn't changed a bit.'*

Nico soaked up the glory, gliding around the room, covering topics of extraordinary difference from armchair upholsterers to the regentrification of London to the investment in property overseas. I felt he could do the job of eldest son for me as well.

He seemed to evolve into whatever skilful managerial role required of him; he settled the will and deeds efficiently. Mother and Aunt Peg would stay on in the house. Debts were paid off. A few personal items were handed out. The family silver, which only made an appearance at Christmas and gave every bite and slurp a metallic taste, was sold. The family-crested plates remained in the pantry with a pair of salt-cellars lined with blue glass, that mother rather liked. I helped myself to a stash of cigarettes and two bottles of Beaujolais and I was surprised to spot a Languedoc-Roussillon wine. There was a small sticky label on the dusty glass neck, it read: *'For Timothy.'* There was no-one else in the family with the name; it was meant for me, although even when I took it from the cellar I had my doubts. I didn't seem to be needed at home so left on an afternoon train. Two days later I had a phone-call at the rectory from mother. I felt I'd been caught out taking the wine, scuttling out of the house without a word, unable to contribute to a house-party of do-gooders. She hadn't realised I'd gone, *"I hadn't realised you'd gone, we'll see you soon then."*

It was hard to fathom whether, *"we'll see you soon,"* was a question or an expectation .

I was invisible when at home and then, when I was gone, there was a small, nagging gap in her wonderings. It was as if a window at the top of the house had been left open causing a draught and had only just been found. That was it, shut it to: closure.

Woof's disappearance and assumed death, only three years after Collioure, was a greater shock. I wrote to Bette and Philly. Their reply was the quickest letter I had ever received, coming within three weeks of my own. Bette was unsteady in her writing. The page was covered in inky blotches and tiny, dried, damp patches. Tears, I guessed. Her words were truly genuine. She felt, *'privileged to have spent some time, however short, with such a dear, young man.'* She would, *'always remember his enthusiasm, his graciousness and* (ironically) *his desire to get the most from life's journey. He was a friend to all, patient and kind but also bold and daring; he listened and he sensed. He will be greatly missed.'*

On reading these lines I had a repeat twinge of that jealousy. I did not wish myself dead, to be honoured with such a eulogy, but to read these qualities run from Bette's pen was to re-open the dark door to my moody heart. How peculiar – where does one's mental state lie at a time like this? To be envious of my dead, young friend because the lady you love, but cannot think of having, writes her soft-hearted, compassionate memory.

Philly signed his name at the end and wrote, *'sending you strength and hope. I shall look to the stars.'*

Then nine months later Bette sent the sad, though not unexpected news, of Claudie's passing.

She was found tucked up in bed with her photo albums lying close beside her, all labelled and in chronological order. A blue ceramic vase holding a faded bunch of mimosa had toppled over, her spirit wished to take a stem of the dry yellow pollen on passing, and to leave by the open window. The water had left a brown stain and Bette mused it had the appearance of the outline of a bull. It was not in my nature to think like this, but it was certainly the way of Bette.

A mournful succession of death and loss. I was 30 years old, in erratic contact with Lymy and Olly, monitoring my drinking and immersed in my work. Bleak but stable.

Part XIII

My tale ends where it began, not in the April of 2016, when I received Bette's final letter, but in the June of the same year. I am 65 years old. I am now custodian in residence of a large house in East Sussex, once owned and lived in by the great British writer, Mr Kipling. The house was bequeathed to our Trust on the death of his widow in 1939, the same year as the outbreak of the Second World War.

I occupy the three, top floor rooms with small, mullioned windows, low Jacobean ceilings and protruding beams and dark-stained panelling. I feel privileged to have the responsibility of one of the finest buildings in our South-Eastern collection. On quiet days I visit the library whose walls are covered with shelves of rare, antique books, lit by the mellow glow of the cleverly-crafted lamps. Upstairs I wander to the writing room with its thick, sturdy oak desk and swivel chair where countless novels were contrived following long, local walks, and put to paper with pen and ink. Close by the fireplace hangs an ethereal, pre-Raphaelite style three-quarter length portrait in oils of Mrs Kipling by the younger Burne-Jones. She is dressed in blue-green with kind, guiding eyes, and a heart and bosom bearing enormous strength. It was a strength well-needed having lost their first-born daughter to pneumonia aged six and, whilst living in Bateman's, the devastating loss of their only son to the carnage of the First World War battlefields. The turn of her body suggests partnership and the urge to instil confidence and instruction. These are some of the wise points of interest I have learnt from Lymy's many visits.

By the end of the 19th century Mr Kipling was the most famous writer in the world and as the new century progressed, counted amongst his friends King George V. Kipling's fame was gathering unwanted and overly inquisitive public attention. Seeking privacy, he decided to move his growing family to a remote country home. Happily, he'd seen the very one for sale, near Etchingham, in Country Life magazine. It was called Bateman's. At first, and sadly for the wealthy writer, the house had only just been purchased, since the magazine he'd read was, inconveniently, six months out of date. However, luck would have it that the soon-to-be owner found the drive from the village road to the house far too hazardous. Pot-holes, sharp wooded corners and steep, slippery inclines meant the horses and cartwheels struggled to make the perilous short ride. Mr Kipling being a forward-thinking man of great determination had acquired a fine set of motor wheels, a Rolls Royce, and a trusted chauffeur. Although the drive was equally bumpy and jerky, Mr Kipling had completely fallen for the peaceful, Arcadian setting. Inspired by the landscape of mixed arable and cattle farming, the fully-functioning family house, nestling in the valley became his home and safe retreat.

It is here I have a modest abode, keeping the original furniture and artefacts in good order, attending to the displays, events and activities; managing those responsible for the upkeep and gardens; sorting the finances and securing the heritage. In spring, I listen out for the first cry of swallows, jotting their arrival date in my wildlife logbook, and for the call of the cuckoo or nightingale from the mill stream beyond the meadow field. In winter the owls from the copse hoot across the hushed lowlands. Through the summer, the birds rehearse to perfection their songs; the beehives buzz and the butterfly varieties flourish. Above the kitchen there is an old dovecote where white doves flap and roost. Most warm early evenings I catch the gentle coo of a wood-pigeon, the great grandfather of all birds. He sits on the hundred-year oak, close to the old car port or perches his portly self on a slender elderflower tree, trying to nip the under-ripe berries. Fed with seeds and grain, they give me much joy these undomesticated birds, with their daily habits and comical customs.

I make time to write, to read, and to let my own history run through my head. I keep a notice board of notes and a few photos. Sometimes I sense, from the 'new authority,' I'm being encouraged to retire, not because - I hasten to add - my work is poor, but merely because there is always a keen-young-someone with 'new ideas' and 'new proposals' who wants to give 'new projects' the dynamic approach. Giving over fallow fields to camp sites during the holidays, for one, or harvesting the kitchen allotment or baking classes at the mill, or book sales in the walled garden. Security is essential. Why only two years ago, an intruder dislodged the two original Elizabethan rose-garden statues. Luckily the gardener had noticed the disturbance and we were able to rescue the figures before they were stolen. They are on display in the garage with the Rolls, locked away at night. Unfortunately, our Trust cannot put *its* trust in society and the good must suffer because of the few bad. I am sceptical of the potential benefits and the proposed forthcoming 'new advances.'

Aunt Peg said once, *"there's a reason one generation makes way for another, be it in resting and retiring or dying and passing on. Each one fails to understand the other's ideas, thoughts and processes. That's God's reason for sending us off."*

She had a point, even if you don't believe it, it's fair to respect it.

She hadn't understood my reason for travelling to France, and once she'd eaten a second chocolate roll, a customary 3 o'clock rant about something topical would begin.

'T'wasn't like that in my day.' She had started her long conversation with this famed rather accusative first line. *'Once upon time,'* was already taken and always sounded much more intriguing.

"Learning was in the classroom, not going on some fancy foreign trip to a foreign place, with their foreign food and funny voices... and what about tea and what about the War, think about that... why all this speaking another language? When will you need it? Only when you go there, and you're not going to go there, coz you're English. Everyone speaks English." She did like to answer her own questions and emphasise the *you* in her phrasing. Would she have angled the issue in quite the same way for someone like Nico, say? Unlikely. Nico had travelled from

New York to Asia to study the varying styles of sky-scrapers. This was so far beyond Aunt Peg's concept of thinking, it came back round full circle, and *his* journey was one of *'quite extraordinary and unbelievable endurance and intelligence.'*

Then she'd wag her fat left finger, because the right hand was busy with a food item or food preparation and end with, *'mark my words.'* *'The End,'* was already taken and it would have been a misnomer to use it. This was not *'The End.'* Another querulous sermon would begin tomorrow and if I happened upon being close it was custom I should give ear to it.

Soon I'll be asked to move over from Kipling's house for the 'new way' to make its impact; whatever it is and whatever it looks like, I won't want to see it, I'll want to move on. Mark my words.

I can hear the echo of Aunt Peg in my head; the inevitability of *'mark my words'* suddenly appearing in my own rhetoric. Should I worry it's arisen earlier in my dialogue than it did with her?

The Kipling house front-door is not the immediate entrance, visitors must first enter from the top garden gate via a small meeting hut. This is where the post is delivered and where several of Bette's letters have met me.

Yesterday, was a June Monday, the 19th already. I took a phone call; an oversized parcel had arrived for me, too bulky for the letterbox. It was sitting at the reception hut and had been sent on, according to a source, from my previous Trust dwelling at Bodiam Castle. I'd been on site at the castle no more than eight months before it was closed for repair work. A routine inspection was carried out, a survey was compiled, contractors were brought in and scaffolding was erected to stabilise most of the weather-beaten exposed interior walls. Olly's son Jimmy, having taken over the majority of the family craft business after Olly's bruising fall from a ladder, ten years previously, came to inspect the masonry and to preserve some of the finer, more intricate features, particularly the stone carvings surrounding the chapel window frames. The Castle was also housing a species of bat, the Daubenton's bat, which held a protective status. The bat preservation society held a small protest, demanding the gateway tower, where the bats were residing, remain untouched during the breeding season, and the months to follow: the noisy, smelly feeding periods. Their wish was granted. I had not been back to the site in a long while. A younger, more modern team of enthusiasts were in charge, embarking on fund-raising projects and filming shoots for television. There was rumour of archery lessons and wine tastings to be included in the programme to entice visitors.

Now, at the public entrance to Bateman's, there was a large *'par avion'* parcel with my name, Mothy Chambers, emblazoned on the brown, creased packaging, the old Bodiam Castle address and then a forwarding address to Kipling's house. The date of the package was November, 2015 and the sender was a *Monsieur Edouard J. Chez Simone Collioure 66190.*

I deduced a Mr J. Edouard had assumed I still lived

at the Castle. He had sent the large item there, where it had taken the present overseer some seven months to forget it. Then suddenly locating my whereabouts they had decided, after this lengthy span, to send it on to the address I had been comfortably settled in for three whole years. It had journeyed a convoluted route. Nonetheless the rectangular, fragile parcel was safe, unopened and in my arms. Who was this *J. Edouard* of Chez Simone? The penmanship was thickly spread and the letters well-defined. Was Simone with Bette? All my thoughts came racing back, my head full of questions. *'My mind as sharp as flint,'* Bette had written in April.

My two Trust colleagues and a local volunteer, busy with the day's chores, were unaware of my excited confusion. Taking the parcel underarm I left, returning to the house via the pathway, around the walled herb garden. The tea-room was preparing lunches, the coffee machine was whizzing and grinding; the gift shop was off-loading a small delivery. I entered the house through a low, staff-only doorway, the little clock above the fireplace in the main entrance hall chimed the midday bells. It sounded cheerful and dutiful and drowned the dull thud of my feet on the stairs.

I took my paper-knife from a side-table, but decided against it, scissors seemed the better option. I took a pair from the kitchen draining board and carefully cut through the sticky paper. Apprehensive, tense, uncertain – I was all these things. Wrapped in brown paper with a soft-cushioning of bubble-wrap, it was tied with string and tape. It took me some time to work through the packaging. I had not felt this young and spirited since a boy on Christmas day. I sensed I was being delivered something of a revelation, something only a long passing of time and a turning over of a generation can hand to you. Although it was not of my heritage, or an heirloom, it would lend a greater significance to the telling of my life's tale. In order, I'll present to you what I opened.

I recognised immediately the framed painting from only glimpsing a small corner of bright oils. Eagerly peeling away the paper, there, in front of me, lay the painting of *'Les Dames Jumelles.'* The one from Les Templiers that had fascinated and mesmerised Bette; the one Philly had later uncharacteristically bought and hung above the mantelpiece, as Bette had explained. I remember picturing the very idea of it; the two quiet, contemplative companion paintings resting side by side in the small front room, above Bette's collection of stones, jewels and personal pieces. Philly would ensure the daylight would not fade the images and Bette would gaze at them every day of her life until – *when did they move?* Bette and Philly had moved from Rue de République on the Faubourg beach side to Rue de Rolland, closer to the market square and more conveniently on a more level path. This time there was no attic, but a small cellar to store boxes. *'The Summer Solstice'* painting had been re-hung but it appears *'Les Dames Jumelles'* was kept well-wrapped in a crate-container. In some way the image had been a distraction for Bette, unable to know of the ladies' whereabouts or even to name them. How incredible it was to see it again: unchanged, unspoiled, unaffected. I had aged. This quiet setting had been captured. It held perpetual beauty, preserving a transient moment in Collioure life. Bette had wanted to discover more about these women but by now, as time rolls on, an interest in their characters would be lessening. Yet history and life have a peculiar and unbeknown ability to re-surface; time does not always mean loss, it can mean new discovery, new light shed upon a subject.

The wooden backing of the painting was insecure, a few hooks had loosened and upset the balance. I knew I must see to its mending. However, inserted behind the painting I'd seen an envelope with my name boldly written on the surface. Here I used the paperknife, which slipped with ease and anxious grace, revealing a long postcard of Collioure and a clear note.

Chez Simone, Collioure

11 Novembre '15

+33 4 34 29 93 47

Dear Mothy,

I'm writing on behalf of my gentil friend, Philly, who I'm so sorry to say is weak and unwell. He says to me to date this message the 11th November, Remembrance Day. Marking important calendar dates was always a habit of Philly's – you may bring this to mind.

I believe we crossed paths once, when I was a little less of two years old. Now I'm a 40-year-old Julian - I can't believe it either! - living in Collioure with maman Simone and taking care of the restaurant.

The enclosed painting is un souvenir, a Christmas gift from Philly. He's not told Bette we send it to you, but says he wants you to own and keep care of it. Now is the right time. It meant a lot, a big deal to her (excuse mon anglais) and it will be a great relief for him to know it is in your hands, on your wall.

I know Bette and you were good friends. I visit Philly and Bette often. Today Bette is out and we have sent this parcel *and correspondence without her knowing. I admit I had to search the house for an address to find you and found Bodiam Castle among a pile of papers in the cave whilst wrapping the painting. I hope it arrives intact. I feel very responsible – maybe you can telephone my number with the news of its safe arrival?*

Philly is rather agitated.

He is adamant there is something you must learn from his lips – these words he wishes you to hear,

'I knew about Bette – she came out of the clouds, as dreams do, that rare full moon, Summer Solstice night. I believed in her. She'll always mean the world and more to me, as you can imagine.'

With my best wishes

Julian

Ps I believe maman is of the same nature as Bette.

Must I clarify further, the last statement left to me from the mouth of Philly and the hand of Julian? Philly had known Bette was from another place, beyond Earth, beyond stars, close to the moon. His mind had been so encouraged by his passion for space and other worldly life, it would not have surprised him; he felt honoured to have her love. Minds meeting on another sphere just as Woof had found with Bette. In a flash, across my brain, flew Woof. I had not thought about him so clearly in a while, it was as if he had pinched my skin. It was not so much a pinch but a prick of conscience. Woof was in this parcel too, somewhere. He had a connection with this foreign and curious adventure. Now it didn't matter who knew what or what had taken place. I soon realised I was the physical point of contact for all four of us. At last I was the key, the intermediary; the one making the associations. As the sun is to the Earth, I was the pivotal point.

I wanted to call Julian but the painting's detached backing was aggravating me. I had the urge to do things in order; job one would be to restore the reverse. I lifted the painting with both hands and held it out front in front of me, absorbing the warmth emanating from the pigments and taking a breath of painted sea-air. I opened a window, there was a scent of freshly mown grass; sounds sprang from all directions, the background to life: twittering birds, giggling school-children. I turned the painting over and a number of useful utensils were within arm's reach – scissors, a screw-driver to lift the stubborn hooks, plyers to remove the slackened ones, brown tape, cotton wool. It seemed more sensible to remove the entire piece and begin again with the attachment. And so, with great precision, I did. What caught my eye caused a sudden gasp and skip of heartbeat. There was a tea-stained piece of paper stuck with tired tape to the white canvas back: an undiscovered and unbeknown hand-written source. It read:

'Les Dames Jumelles' by Jeffery Barker

My wife and her sister arrived in Collioure, 21st *of June, 1948*

Pour La Famille Pous à Les Templiers.

A Monsieur Barker, or Mr Barker, his name was English, mixing a little French into the wording. Jeffrey Barker was married to one of the beautifully, idealised and idolised women. Was it the one with un chapeau paille, reading her book, contemplating, or the other, running her hands through her green necklace, seeking shade from the intense balcony heat? I know the name Jeffrey Barker, so do you, it is on these pages you have leafed through. Jeffrey Barker is Woof's full name, but this painting cannot be by him, he was born three years later, in 1951, like me. I can only assume it is his father, and one of the fine ladies is his mother, and one his aunt. Bette said she had known them once, long ago. They had taken voyage as she had; they had reminded her of Simone and herself. Was this why Bette and Woof had shared an otherworldly and rarefied level of understanding? The spiritual sphere, I have often called it.

Today is Tuesday, I have not slept a wink. I listened to the clock toll every hour's bell. The sun rose early, flooding the darkest corners of the bedroom with a strong, beckoning light. It was 4.15am. I have tossed and turned my musings as a consequence of yesterday's marvellous rebirth and found I even woke with a crescent-moon smile tipping the corners of my mouth. The previous evening I'd taken a good stiff whisky and a stroll around the inner gardens. I smoked two, much-craved cigarettes beside the lily-pond; all my cigarettes are much-needed because I have unwillingly reduced their numbers. I avoided a circus-mirror reflection in the water but childishly began lifting the silky, emerald-green lily-pads to watch speckled goldfish dart and slip away. I had hung *'Les Dames Jumelles'* in my small sitting room and felt embraced by an atmosphere of peace and enormous gladness.

It was late in the day. I'd taken a nap, completed some paper-work, seen to a damp issue in Mr Kipling's garage, and checked the level of mill-pond water. I knew I had to make the phone call to Julian; it bothers me I have left it so long. Running a few lines through my head, imagining a rush-hour of hungry eaters at Chez Simone. I called twice. After a long dialling tone, wishing to speak to Julian, I gave my name.

It took some minutes to locate him and he was breathless at the receiver. *"Pardon, je suis desolé! Une combinasion de chaleur et de vitesse!"*

I explained, in English, about the lost parcel and address. It was an awkward telephone apology. I sensed there was so much to say to one another that nothing sensible could be said at all. Too much time had gone by, the weather and one's health were the safest topics of conversation, until I said,

"Is Bette with you... is Bette there?"

Julian replied in a calm, clear, distinct voice, something I had appreciated in his writing.

"Bette just left, she said she was 'going home.' It's a full-moon Summer Solstice tonight."

Of course, it was Tuesday 20th June 2016.

"There won't be another one like it, not in our lifetime. 2062 will be the next occurrence. A moment of change, a new beginning. Who knows what Ather will bring to Earth then." Silence ensued.

"Au-revoir mon ami," Julian whispered to me down a phone-line that transported me over 800 miles to a small, magical town on the Mediterranean coast of France. A town where boats bobbed, people lived and died and a special woman was, tonight, going home.

I knew I would not see Julian or Collioure again.

I watched the sun start its descent as a great full moon rose over the far meadow field. As the evening went on I could feel le clocher bells beat with my heart. I toasted Bette and Philly and dear, young, funny Woof.

"By sharing your lives with me you gave my life meaning. You gave me a story and by doing so, you saved me. See you in the sky, my friends!"

The End, La Fin

Lightning Source UK Ltd.
Milton Keynes UK
UKOW01f1937040318
318852UK00001B/1/P

9 780993 581755